A CENTURY
OF STORIES
NEW HANOVER COUNTY PUBLIC LIBRARY
1906-2006

If I Have a
Wicked Stepmother,
Where's My Prince?

MELISSA KANTOR

HYPERION
NEW YORK

First Edition
1 3 5 7 9 10 8 6 4 2
Printed in the United States of America
Reinforced binding

Library of Congress Cataloging-in-Publication Data on file.
ISBN 0-7868-0960-4

Visit www.hyperionteens.com

To Carol Einhorn

Chapter One

Cinderella	Me
dead mother	dead mother
wicked stepmother	wicked stepmother
evil stepsisters (2)	evil stepsisters (2)
friendless	friendless

I tapped my pen against my lips, debating whether or not
Cinderella is actually friendless. I mean, she does have all
those talking animals helping her out when she gets into
a jam. But do they count as friends? It's not as if a blue
jay can meet you at Starbucks for an after-school latte. As
I tried to categorize the small woodland creatures Cinderella associates with, my eyes accidentally wandered
over to Jessica Johnson, this girl who sits across the classroom from me. When we made eye contact, her expression didn't change—it was as though I wasn't there.

I crossed out *friendless* in the Cinderella column and drew in a woodchuck.

Cinderella	Me
father dead	father alive

Once more, I wasn't sure this was an accurate description of our respective situations. I mean, technically, my dad is alive. More than technically—it's not like he's in a coma or anything. But considering that I am currently living with his new wife and stepdaughters on Long Island while he spends Monday to Friday back in San Francisco finishing up this mondo case he was supposed to be done with before we moved to New York in August *seven months ago*, his being alive doesn't do me a whole lot of good.

I went back to my list and put quotation marks around *alive*.

" . . . that you can't subtract *here* until you divide *here*." Mr. Palmer slapped the board, raising a small cloud of chalk dust. Then he spun toward the window. "*Mister* Marcus," he spat. "Can you tell me *why* that is?"

John Marcus's head shot up and he looked around the room in a panic. The skateboarding magazine tucked into his math book slipped to the floor.

I barely listened as Mr. Palmer raged at John, spit flying out of the corners of his mouth. I wasn't the only one unimpressed by Mr. Palmer's tantrum (his third of the day); even John kept his eyes on his magazine, sliding it under his chair with his toe. And as usual, even before the bell had rung, despite the fact that Mr. Palmer was still talking, kids started throwing stuff into their backpacks. "I *think* you're going to want to hear this since it involves a possible *surprise quiz* on Thursday." No one paid any attention to him. Mr. Palmer is always threatening surprise quizzes and then not giving them. All first semester I spent my nights cramming frantically for a quiz that never came. Now I just ignored his threats like everyone else.

Out in the hallway, Madison Lawler, Jessica Johnson's BFF, embraced Jessica passionately, as if the cruelty of the math-tracking powers that be was almost too much to bear. Maybe I'm paranoid, but as I walked by, it was hard not to feel that the sole purpose of their daily reunion was to remind me of my utterly friendless state.

For the record, let's just acknowledge that relocation has not done wonders for my social life. To say I haven't discovered a soul mate within the Glen Lake population would be an understatement. I have not even discovered a homework mate. And the irony of my current situation is that I *just went through this a year ago.* When I was in eighth grade, my dad got totally obsessed with how the curriculum at my junior high wasn't rich enough or enriched enough or *whatever,* and he decided that if I didn't attend Wellington Academy for high school, mine would be an empty and meaningless existence (kind of like it is now). So I had to kiss Bayview Middle School good-bye, leave all my friends, and go off to Wellington, where I knew no one. Then, just as I'm finally settling in and can stop skulking around the halls like an assassin, practically at the very moment my cell phone starts ringing with calls from people who don't just want me to switch my long-distance carrier, my dad announces he's getting married to the Wicked Witch of the North Shore, we're moving to New York, and I'll be starting sophomore year at Glen Lake High in the fall.

You know who people don't stay in touch with when she leaves their time zone?

The new girl.

I made my way to my locker and then to the cafeteria. Since January, when I started taking studio art, I've usually been able to eat my lunch in the art room, thereby avoiding the humiliation of being the lone occupant of a cafeteria table that could easily seat twenty. But Ms. Daniels, my art teacher, was holding private conferences in the studio all through lunch today, so I had nowhere to flee. I bought a sandwich and made my way to what seemed to be an isolated, undesirable table in the corner of the crowded lunchroom.

It turned out I was wrong about the table's undesirability, just as I've been wrong about pretty much everything else at Glen Lake High. Within minutes of my sitting down at one end, a noisy group of seniors swarmed and then sat at the other, twirling car keys around their index fingers and grabbing French fries out of one another's McDonald's bags.

In the center of the crowd sat Connor Pearson, laughing and chatting with his loyal subjects. The star of the basketball team and president of the student council, Connor was also voted "Best Looking" by the senior class. In the fall, to raise money, the cheerleaders raffled off a kiss with Connor Pearson and *two hundred* girls bought tickets. (That would be one hundred and ninety-nine girls plus yours truly.) But sadly for me and all the other members of Glen Lake's female population, rumor was Connor only had eyes for Kathryn Ford: Homecoming Queen, who, like all good queens, was currently seated to the right of her lordship.

Some people make me feel freakishly taller and redder-headed than I actually am, and Kathryn Ford is one of those people. Everything about her is tiny and pale and perfect. I think she might have been created from a kit. Also, she acts as though ignoring underclassmen is a varsity sport.

Basically, you can't not hate her.

Still, I'm not crazy enough to think it's Kathryn Ford's fault that Connor Pearson doesn't know I exist. Or that she's blacklisted me, and that's why I have yet to make one friend within the Glen Lake community. I know I have only myself to blame. I watch the kids in my classes talking before the bell rings, and I know all I need to do if I want to talk to them is *talk*. Just say something. *Anything*. And it's not like I don't want to talk to some of them. It's not as if it's *their* fault I was dragged kicking and screaming across the continental United States.

If three's supposed to be the charm, it hasn't made me especially charming. Moving to New York to attend my third school in three years appears to have mutated some friend-making gene I didn't even know I had. Now, instead of talking to people like I normally would, I just sit silently, as if I'm watching them swing a jump rope higher and higher while waiting for just the right moment to step in and start jumping.

And it never comes.

That night at dinner, while I was just sitting there minding my own business and trying to decide if I should take my dad up on his wager that the Rockets were going to lose by ten, one of my twelve-year-old twin stepsisters looked over at me and pursed her lips, as if I were something she'd eaten and didn't like the taste of. I should have taken her look as a warning, but I was too busy calculating the game's odds. Which is why a minute later, when she addressed me, I was caught totally off guard.

"You should wear a padded bra, Lucy," said Princess One, still eyeing me. "Your boobs are *really* small."

Unfortunately she hadn't cleared this tip with her sister, who was so eager to offer counter advice, she nearly choked on her veggie burger. "It's too late for that *now*," said Princess Two. "She should have started back in September."

"That's a good point," acknowledged Princess One.

Neither one of my stepsisters seemed at all bothered by the fact that compared to them, I'm Pamela Anderson.

"Actually," I said, "you know how last week you said I should get blond highlights because of how my hair's too red?"

The Princesses nodded eagerly.

"Well, I was thinking I'd dye my boobs blond and get a padded skull."

"Ha ha, Lucy," said Princess One. "News flash: Maybe if you took this kind of thing a little more seriously, you would have been invited to the homecoming dance."

"News flash," I echoed. "Not everyone's life goal is to get the word JUICY tattooed on her ass."

"Lucy," Mara said, emerging from the coma she enters whenever her daughters start criticizing me, "please don't use that kind of language at the table."

After dinner I headed down to my "room," known in most houses as "the basement."

For the first few months after my dad and I moved into my stepmother's house, I was actually a little worked up about the fact that I live in a furnitureless dungeon where my "bed" is an air mattress; and my clothing—which was initially in cardboard "dressers"— has slowly ended up in piles all over the floor, as first one and then another and then yet another of the "drawers" fell apart. Each time I had the temerity to complain, to point out that the only reason I didn't bring my old furniture from San Francisco to New York was because of all the beautiful new stuff Mara was "so excited" to buy, I was reminded by my stepmother, the amateur interior decorator, that finding the "perfect piece" takes time. Nations have fallen and risen, revolutions have come and gone, celebrity couples have wed and divorced, and still the right headboard eludes my stepmother.

The one cool thing about being down here is I put up posters of my two favorite paintings; except for them the walls are completely bare, so it's kind of like being in a museum—you know, vast empty space punctuated by spectacular works of art. Lying on my "bed" I can either look at the wall across from me, where Matisse's *The Dancer* hangs, or up at the ceiling, where I've tacked a ginormous poster of *Autumn Rhythm (Number 30)*.

My mom was a really great artist. Her paintings hang in museums all over Europe, and MOMA and the Metropolitan Museum of Art each own one. The walls of our house in San Francisco were covered with her work, but when we moved we put it all in storage. My dad said Mara's feelings might be hurt if we asked to hang Mom's paintings here. That's pretty much the major theme in my life now—Mara's feelings. Basically, they're always being hurt or in danger of being hurt.

Which means I'm always in trouble or in danger of being in trouble.

Before I went to sleep, I flipped through a book of Cezanne reproductions I'd gotten out of the library. But even staring at his perfect pears, each one so sculpted and weighty, I couldn't get my mind off the list I'd been making in math, the proof that something had gone very, very wrong with my life.

Because if I have a wicked stepmother and two evil stepsisters, aren't I supposed to get a prince?

Chapter Two

Once upon a time I actually tried to make a friend at Glen Lake.

This was back in January, at the start of second semester, when I was foolishly convinced my life was about to turn around. I'd signed up for this art class, and from the first day I could tell it was going to be great. Unlike the rest of the Glen Lake faculty, Ms. Daniels, the art teacher, A) really knows her stuff, B) is not deaf, dumb, blind and/or clinically insane, and C) does not dress as if we were still living under President Washington. Plus, she's not afraid to give serious assignments (still lifes, nudes) and to grade them *hard*.

The other kids in the class aren't especially talented, except for one, Sam Wolff, a junior who's without a doubt the best artist in the whole school. His paintings hang all over the building, and when Ms. Daniels took attendance on the first day of class and I realized he was the guy whose art I'd been admiring all first semester, I was totally psyched. Finally, someone I could talk to about something I loved.

The second week of class, when I got to the studio early and found him alone, sitting and sketching on the old couch in the corner, I figured, *Now's my chance.* I tried to start up a conversation, telling him how much I liked a still life he did that was on display in the lobby. It's a painting of one of those small green tables they have at Starbucks, and on the table there's a coffee cup, a crumpled napkin, some change, and a half-eaten doughnut. Even though he played with proportions and perspective, somehow everything seems incredibly real. You can feel the grains of sugar spilled on the table's surface and the sticky icing on the doughnut.

I told Sam I thought the painting was really cool and I'd spent a long time looking at it. I told him how it seemed like you could just take a bite of the doughnut. For the first seven eighths of my monologue, he just squinted up at me, not saying anything. Then, after I'd been going on and on for, like, two hours, he put on his glasses (he wears these glasses with thick, black rims), stopped squinting, and said, "Thanks." But he didn't say it like, *Thanks, it's really cool of you to take time out from your busy schedule to appreciate the art I have labored to create. Just knowing my work is appreciated is all the gratitude I need from this cruel, cruel world.*

Instead, he said it like, *Could you possibly crawl back into whatever hole you crawled out of and stop bothering me?*

Needless to say, I have stopped pursuing friendship within the Glen Lake artistic community.

On Wednesday, I spent all of art finishing up a charcoal still life of a glass of water, a lemon, and a notebook on a shelf by an open window. When the bell rang I headed to my drawer to put my stuff away, and Ms. Daniels gestured at me to come over to where she was culling the most ancient tubes of paint from a cupboard and chucking them in the trash. She flipped open a tube, tested the paint on the back of her hand, then returned it to the shelf before taking my drawing from me.

"This is looking good, Lucy," she said, tracing her finger along the edge of the page. "I love how diaphanous the curtains are."

"Thanks," I said. I was really proud of the curtains; I'd drawn just the edges and a few lines to indicate folds; I wanted the fabric to seem material but weightless.

She handed back the sketch and put her hands together in front of her chin, tapping her index fingers against her lips. "Lucy, do you know Francesco Clemente?"

Ms. Daniels and I have talked a lot about different artists we like, but I'd never heard of Clemente. I was tempted to pretend I knew who he was so I wouldn't disappoint her, but at the last second I changed my mind. I mean, what if he wasn't even an artist? What if he was the Prime Minister of Spain or something?

I shook my head. "Who is he?"

She wrapped her long hair into a loose bun at the base of her neck. "He's an artist here in New York," she said. "His stuff is just extraordinary. It actually reminds me of Picasso's later work. All that talent and joy." She slipped a pencil through the bun to hold it in place. "He has a retrospective at the Guggenheim. You should check it out."

I wondered if she'd told anyone else about his show or just me. Since January I'd wanted Ms. Daniels to think my work was somehow special. Was this the sign I'd been waiting for? Without my even being conscious of it, I felt the corners of my lips edging upward, something that hadn't happened in a long, long time. It was sort of a miracle my smile muscles hadn't atrophied. Thinking out loud, I said, "Maybe I'll go." I could ask my dad if he wanted to go, too. Of course that meant I couldn't go *this* Saturday. This Saturday had been reserved by Mara to be spent in pursuit of her own personal holy grail: the late American-Victorian breakfront without which the front hallway looks, and I quote, "as if nobody *loves* it!"

"Clemente's painting is just thrilling," Ms. Daniels said. "And I think you'll find it particularly interesting in terms of the direction your art is taking."

My art was taking a *direction*?

13

"Sounds amazing," I said, making the decision to go right then and there. "I won't miss it. Thanks."

I thought Ms. Daniels's compliment would at least carry me through the week, but no sooner had I pushed open the door to the cafeteria than the chill of social exile penetrated the warm fuzzy feeling I'd gotten talking to her. I bought a turkey sandwich and grabbed a chair at an empty table where someone had left today's sports section. Reading about basketball might have cheered me up if there hadn't been a front-page article about how the Lakers were guaranteed to lose to Chicago tonight. My dad grew up in L.A., and I was born there. So even though I've lived most of my life in San Francisco, I'm a *huge* Lakers fan. As if the gloomy article wasn't bad enough, who should decide to sit in the empty seats just down the table from me but Jessica and Madison.

"Okay, can I just *show* you the bear?" asked Madison. "Because you're going to *die*!" I glanced over at them. Madison's subtly highlighted hair was pulled back in a sleek ponytail, and her lips were a plummy color I knew even my stepsisters would approve.

Jessica finished ripping the foil off her yogurt and looked up at Madison. "Give," she said, reaching out her hand and wiggling her fingers.

Madison looked like she was about to explode with happiness as she handed Jessica the bear. "You have to *squeeze* it," Madison explained.

Jessica squeezed the bear, which announced, "I love you."

Madison gave a little cry of excitement, like she'd been waiting an eternity for just such a confession from this particular bear. "I know it's completely dumb," she said. "But it's so cute."

"You guys are nauseating," said Jessica, but she said it in a nice way, like she didn't really mind having a friend who was one half of a nauseating couple.

"Thanks," said Madison. "I was telling him that since it's our three-month anniversary, he should—" Suddenly she pointed across the cafeteria. "Hey," she shouted. Then she started waving her arms. I glanced in the direction she was waving and saw Matt and Dave, Madison and Jessica's boyfriends, walking toward the table we were all sitting at.

With them was Connor Pearson.

I stared at him as he crossed the room. It was like my eyes were acting of their own accord; they couldn't not admire Connor's long legs and broad shoulders, his graceful, athlete's walk. And who could blame them? If Michelangelo's *David* strolled out of L'Academia wearing a Glen Lake High School Basketball jacket, you'd stare, too.

When the guys got to the table, Madison jumped up and gave Matt a PG-defying kiss. As if inspired by their peers' passion, Jessica and Dave started making out with equal, if imitative, lust.

Finally Madison pulled away and slapped Matt on the upper arm. "I hate Matt," she said in a little girl voice.

"Whoa," he said, mock rubbing his arm. "What's that for?"

"For watching the game with these guys tonight instead of seeing a movie with me," she said. "Matt. Is. A. Jerk." She pounded him on the chest with each word.

"You don't understand," Dave explained to Madison as Matt warded off her blows. "This is going to be *the* game. L.A.'s going *down*." He and Matt high-fived.

And then, out of nowhere, as if support for the home team is some kind of autonomic response, I muttered, "Yeah, right."

As soon as I realized what I'd done, I tried to focus my eyes on my paper, like the words I'd spoken had been elicited not by my eavesdropping but by something I'd read. Only it was too late. Dave, Matt, Connor, Jessica, and Madison were all staring at me as if I were a piece of furniture that had suddenly been given the power of speech.

"Are you crazy?" said Dave. "Did you see the way Chicago played last night?"

I gave up trying to avert my eyes and looked at him. "How'd they play?" I asked. "The Lakers' two best players were out and the ref called five totally insane fouls. Chicago was *handed* the game."

"Handed the game?" Dave was practically choking with indignation. He dropped his arm from Jessica's shoulders. "Did you see that three-pointer at the buzzer? Did you?"

"I saw it," I said.

"Then what are you *talking* about?" He reached out like he wanted to shake me.

"Hey, easy there, man," Connor said, grabbing Dave's arm and holding on until he dropped it back to his side.

Dave and I kept glaring at each other, but if the only thing rattling Dave was my saying Chicago was going down, I was freaking about way more than that. Speaking without being spoken to constituted a major social taboo.

I was royally screwed.

Just as Jessica opened her mouth to say something to me (no doubt along the lines of, *Shut up, Freak!*), Connor let go of Dave's arm and turned in my direction. "Sorry about that," he said. "The D-Man gets a little passionate about Chicago."

And then he winked at me.

Connor Pearson winked at me.

Everyone saw it, too, and I felt myself getting warm. "Yeah, sure," I stuttered. "Don't worry about it."

Jessica shut her mouth and turned away. Because when Connor Pearson winks at someone, that someone isn't royally screwed.

She's royally pardoned.

"Yo, Pearson!" We all looked over to the door where Kathryn Ford and two of her attendants stood. Even from across the room her smile was blinding. "Are you coming or what?"

"You know it," Connor shouted back. He turned to Dave and Matt. "Come on, guys," he said.

Dave and Jessica, Matt and Madison started making out again. It seemed nothing would put an end to their lip locks, until Conner grabbed the sleeve of Dave's jacket and started pulling. "Let's go!" he said, yanking hard at the leather. And then Dave was pulling on Matt's jacket and suddenly—*poof!*—all three of them were gone.

No one said anything for a minute after the guys left, and then Jessica turned in my direction.

"Wow, you're really, like, into basketball, aren't you?"

Could that be curiosity in her tone? *Hey, you're the new girl who's in my math class. I've really let far too much time go by without getting to know you better. Tell us about your passion for sport!* I was unfamiliar with the social norms of my new habitat—was she friend or foe?

"Yeah," I said. I hated that my answer was so meek, as if I was waiting to see whether she approved of it. I sat up straighter. "I'm a *huge* fan." I was prepared to defend my leisure activity to the death.

This, apparently, would not be necessary. "Cool," said Jessica. Then she turned from me to Madison. "Did you see Connor and Kathryn in the senior parking lot this morning?"

"Oh my god," said Madison. "I give it a month, tops, before they get together."

"A month?" said Jessica. "Try a week. You should have heard her. She was all, 'I heard the Knicks are having a great season,' and he was all, 'This could be their year.'"

"Like Kathryn suddenly cares about basketball," said Madison.

"Like *anyone* cares about basketball," said Jessica. And she bit down emphatically on a baby carrot.

I wanted to say something about the pleasures of basketball, what it's like to lose yourself in a really great game, to watch your team come up from behind to score an unexpected victory, to see a player you've been doubting for months suddenly find his rhythm. There was so much I could have said.

But I'd already said more than enough. I finished my sandwich and the article and gathered up my trash, not surprised that neither Jessica nor Madison acknowledged my leaving.

Chapter Three

When it was just me and my dad, we used to eat at any old time, but as far as Mara's concerned, if you don't sit down to a hot meal at seven on the dot, you're some kind of irredeemable savage. And "sitting down to a meal" doesn't just mean sitting down. It means china, silver, candles, and elaborate floral arrangements. Mara quit her "job" (as a part-part-part-time PR consultant) about fifteen seconds after my dad proposed, so now she's free to expend massive quantities of time and energy obsessing about important food-related accessories, such as crème brulée ramekins and something called *demitasse* spoons. Once, she walked into the kitchen when I was eating lo mein directly out of the carton with my fingers; she gasped and put her hand to her chest as if she'd found me gnawing on a human head.

As usual no one said much to me all through

dinner—Mara and the Princesses just compared theories about celebrity couples and upcoming fashion trends. I couldn't exactly be upset about being ignored since my other option was to be enlightened about the ways I am physically and/or sartorialy repulsive.

After dinner the phone rang, just like it does every night at eight. I was standing right by it holding a pile of dishes I'd carried in from the dining-room table. I dumped the dishes in the sink and grabbed the receiver.

"Hey, Goose, how's it going?" asked my dad when I answered.

"Okay," I said.

"How was school?"

Even though my dad asks me that every time we talk, I can tell he doesn't really want to know the truth. I mean, who wants to hear his daughter is a social pariah? Instead of lingering on the gory details of my unsocial life, I told him how Connor, Dave, and Matt thought Chicago was going to beat L.A.

"Wow, those Glen Lake kids really *are* stupid," he said.

"Not to mention totally gross," I said, and I launched into a description of the make-out session I'd witnessed at lunch. Halfway through my verbal rendition of the couples' game of doubles tonsil-tennis, Princess One, who was sitting with her sister at the kitchen table IM-ing boys across the tri-state area from their mother's laptop, interrupted.

"Are you talking about Jessica Johnson?" she asked.

"Wait, hold on," I said to my dad. I turned around. "What?"

"I *said* are you talking about Jessica Johnson? Because she's totally awesome," she said.

I heard my dad calling my name through the receiver. "Hang on a sec," I said, still looking at Princess One. "How do you know Jessica Johnson?" I asked.

Princess Two sighed and blew a stream of air up at her bangs. "Hel-*lo*! She's only, like, Jennifer's older sister." Jennifer, I had been informed recently, is the name of the girl who's currently the Princesses' best friend. Like the chairmanship of the European Union, this position rotates periodically.

"Wait a second, you're telling me there are parents around here whose last name is Johnson who actually named their children Jennifer and Jessica? What's their brother's name, Jack?"

"Jason," the Princesses said in unison.

I started laughing. "What?" they asked, looking at me.

"You don't think it's kind of stupid to give all your kids names that begin with the same letter as their last name?" I asked.

"*I* like it," said Princess Two. "It's *classy*."

I was about to say it was as classy as a porn star, but by now my dad was practically screaming my name.

"Sorry," I said, putting the receiver back up

to my ear. "I just had to navigate some Long Island lunacy."

When my dad and Mara decided to get married, there was this whole debate about where we should live. Because the Princesses' dad lives the next town over *and* they have about twice as much time left in school as I do, the decision was made that my dad and I would depart San Francisco rather than subjecting the Princesses to a potentially traumatic relocation across the Mississippi River. If you ask me, this was a huge mistake, since leaving the 516-area code is the only thing that could have saved my stepsisters from growing up to be Humvee-driving, acrylic-nail wearing, soap-opera addicted housewives.

Unfortunately for them, nobody asked me.

"So," said my dad, "did you see the *Times*? Stanford's looking pretty good. I think this could be their year." My dad, who went to Stanford, has a loyalty to his alma mater that I can only describe as perverse. In spite of the fact that their team has not even made it close to the NCAA finals in decades, he continues to bet on them year after year.

Before I could answer, I heard a click, which meant Mara had picked up the extension in the den. It's this totally annoying thing she does—getting on the phone with me and my dad. It's like she's afraid if she doesn't supervise him every second, he'll realize what a mistake he made marrying her.

"Hello, darling," she said.

"Hi, honey," he said.

Gag me.

I did what I always do when Mara butts in on our conversations: I ignored her.

"It's only February," I said to my dad. "I can't start thinking NCAA yet."

"Wait," said Mara. "I just got used to NBA. What's NCAA?"

My dad laughed as though Mara had just said the most amusing thing he'd ever heard. "We'll cross that bridge when we come to it, Mrs. Norton," he said, still chuckling. "Sweetheart, you are officially cute."

I cleared my throat to remind him he wasn't exactly having a private conversation.

"Lucy, I'm just telling you," he said, "Stanford is having a killer season."

I groaned. The truth is, even if I thought Stanford had a chance of winning the NCAA, which they don't, I could never root for the school that is responsible for my current state of misery. Had my father and Mara's brother not been on the same floor together freshman year at Stanford, and had Mara's brother not decided to look up his old classmate two years ago when he had business in San Francisco, and had my dad not, shortly thereafter, had a conference at his firm's New York office, and had he, after that conference, not met his old classmate for a drink, and had his old classmate not

24

brought his divorced sister to said drink, and had said old classmate's sister not been *totally* on the prowl for a new husband, and had my dad not fallen for a woman who thinks interior decorating is a liberal art, I would not currently be living in social exile, related by marriage to twelve-year-old twins who believe getting a cut and color is a spiritually enriching experience.

"Stanford's going down, Dad. Take a reality check." It may have been cold comfort that Stanford had zero chance of taking the NCAA title, but it was comfort nonetheless.

"It's incredible," said Mara. "If you had told me a year ago that I'd have a daughter who was a sports fanatic, I never would have believed it."

I didn't say anything. If you ask me, it's totally weird how she's started referring to me as her daughter. This summer, right before they got married, Mara took me out for dinner and gave me this whole speech about how she would never try to replace my mother and how she totally understood I could never love her the way I had loved my real mother, but she hoped she could play a role in my life. I told her that I didn't really remember my real mom all that well considering she died of cancer when I was only three, so it wasn't exactly like there was anything to replace. I *meant* I didn't really feel like I *needed* a mother, but it's become clear that Mara thinks I meant I wanted *her* to be my mother.

"*MOM!*" screeched the Princesses.

"What is it?" I could hear Mara in both my right ear, through the phone, and in my left, from the den. She was everywhere at once.

"We *need* you!"

"Coming." I heard the click of the phone as she hung it up

"Hey, Dad," I said, taking advantage of our having a minute to talk without Mara listening in. "You want to go to the Guggenheim with me next Saturday?"

"Sure, Goose. That would be fun. We haven't been to a museum in a while."

I couldn't believe how easy that had been. Why hadn't I suggested we do something alone together before?

Mara came running into the kitchen. "Yes, girls?"

"Never mind," said Princess One, not bothering to look up from the screen. "It's working now."

Mara wasn't even mad that she'd run all the way across the house for nothing. She just walked over to where I was still on the phone.

"Lucy, could you finish helping to clear the table?" I loved how she said "helping," like anyone besides me was doing it.

"Well, bye, Dad," I said, taking Mara's not-so-subtle hint.

"Bye, Goose. See you tomorrow." I gave Mara the phone and headed into the dining room, where I discovered neither of the Princesses had cleared so much as a fork from her place. When I went back into the kitchen carrying their stuff, I almost made a joke about how Cinderella should know better than to think her stepsisters might actually clean up after themselves, but I knew nobody but me would think it was funny.

People never think things that are true are funny.

Chapter Four

"Lucy, I just know we're going to find some *lovely* furniture for your room on this trip. I'm *sooo* glad you could come with us today."

It was Saturday morning, and we were walking along the main street of Lomax, New York, a Hudson River Valley town that's cute with a capital K. Every place we passed was either a bed and breakfast or an antique furniture store. When we first arrived, I'd asked a salesman at Jane's Junk and Valuables if there was a place in town that sold CDs, and he looked at me like I'd inquired about purchasing a hand-held rocket grenade launcher.

"Doug, honey, look at this." Mara pulled my father toward a picture window that held a gigantic piece of furniture I now knew was called a breakfront. "Wouldn't that just look yummy in the foyer?"

"It's nice, sweetheart," said my dad. "You want to go inside and have a look at it?"

Mara's eyes lit up. "How do you know me so well? Of *course* I do." He held the door open for her and she practically danced across the threshold. (At least he didn't carry her.)

"You coming, Goose?" asked my dad. He asked like I had a choice, like if I said no I wouldn't be accused of Having a Bad Attitude. Apparently if you don't think examining ancient wooden furniture in tiny little towns is just the dandiest way to spend your free time, you Have a Bad Attitude. You also Hurt Mara's Feelings, which is a very, very bad thing to do. That's why I was stuck on today's little outing—because last weekend, instead of lying and saying I had a lot of friends or work or *anything* that might keep me from spending my day comparing late-early Victorian breakfronts with early-late Victorian breakfronts, I had made the catastrophic error of admitting I'm just not all that into furniture shopping. That was last Saturday morning. Last *Sunday* morning, my dad came into my room and told me that Mara's feelings were very, very hurt, and he certainly hoped I'd reconsider and come with them next weekend. Even though he used the word *hope* he clearly meant *know* as in, "I know you'll reconsider and come with us next weekend, or you will be grounded for the rest of your life."

I told him I was looking forward to joining them.

I followed Mara into the store. "Look around, Goose," said my dad. "Maybe you'll find something you like for your room."

As if it weren't bad enough that I was living in a furniture-free zone, Mara had added insult to injury by basically redoing the entire house in the seven months since we moved in. I once made the mistake of asking my dad if it didn't strike him as being just the tiniest bit suspicious that she'd been able to select, order, and *have shipped from England* an entire living-room set while continuing to claim that there was not a single chest of drawers in the entire New York metropolitan area worthy of my basement bedroom. My dad just got really stern and said, "What are you implying, Lucy? That Mara doesn't *want* to furnish your room?" Actually that was exactly what I'd been implying, but watching him get like that, all cold and scary, totally freaked me out. So I just said, "Nothing. I'm not implying anything," and never mentioned it again.

I pretended to be looking at a dresser roughly the size of the Arc de Triomphe while Mara squealed with pleasure over the breakfront. Finally her cries of excitement ("Look, honey, a *tiny drawer!*") were more than I could take, and I made my way to the back of the store, where furniture was piled so crazily it was almost impossible to find a space to stand. Then my eyes hit on something that actually got my attention—in a good way.

"Dad! Hey, Dad! Check this out." It must have taken my dad about twenty minutes to respond; no doubt it's pretty hard to pull yourself away from a scintillating breakfront tête à tête.

"Yeah?" he finally answered.

"Make a left," I said. "I'm right around the corner where the little table is."

"Wow, this is terra incognita," said my dad, climbing over a footstool.

"And look what I discovered," I said. Leaning against the wall was an old-fashioned wooden easel. The chain that attached the legs was delicately wrought filigree, and the wood itself was a dark cherry, carved everywhere in an intricate pattern. It looked like an easel Monet or Ingres might have used. "Pretty cool, huh?" I said.

"Oh, yeah," he said. "It's amazing." He knelt down. "Look at this." He pointed toward the floor.

"Wow." I hadn't noticed that the legs ended in tiny, carved lion paws. "That's beautiful."

Kneeling in the dim light of the antique shop, I realized this was probably the first time in almost a year I was actually getting a minute alone with my dad. So it didn't exactly come as a surprise when I heard Mara calling his name.

"Doug? Doug, where are you?" Her tone bordered on frantic.

"In the back, honey," he called, standing up. "Make a left at the marble table."

"It's so dusty back here."

Mara prefers her antiques nice and clean. It's okay that furniture's *been* used, as long as it doesn't *look* used.

"Look what Lucy found," my dad said, pointing at the easel. "Isn't it amazing?"

Mara made a bright face. "Oh, it's lovely!" she said. "What a nice piece. It's like something you'd find in a museum."

Right then I knew I'd never be allowed to get the easel. If Mara had just said it was nice, maybe there'd be a chance, but "It's like something you'd find in a museum" translated to "This comes into the house over my dead body."

My dad didn't get it at first. "Oh, you like it?" he asked.

"I love it," she said, nodding energetically. "It's really a shame we don't have a place for such an original piece."

Unlike my dad, I got where Mara was going with her faux enthusiasm, but I couldn't believe she was really prepared to walk away from something so beautiful. "I thought it could go in my room," I said.

Mara's nodding turned to head shaking and she smiled a sad smile. "I hear what you're saying, Lucy. I just don't think it's quite right for the space."

Yeah, 'cause you wouldn't want to buy something *that would clash with* nothing.

"Well, maybe we could work around it. You know, you could pick furniture that would match it somehow."

"Mmmm, yeah." She pursed her lips, like she was thinking really hard about what I was saying. "Unfortunately, I just don't think that's going to work."

"Well, why not?" I asked. My voice came out sharper than I'd meant it to.

My dad, who had been examining the scrollwork at the base of the easel, looked up. I could tell he'd been too engrossed in the carving to hear a word that was said until now, so as far as he was concerned, I was taking this edgy tone with Mara for no reason at all.

"Lucy, I know you're disappointed," she said. "But right now we really have to focus on the essentials."

She turned and made her way to the front of the store. My dad put his hand on my shoulder. "Maybe another time, Goose," he said.

"Yeah, maybe," I said.

While my dad paid for the breakfront and Mara and the salesman set up a good day to have it delivered, I stood by the door, idly thinking about the only good thing that had happened to me recently—that wink I'd gotten from Connor Pearson. I was still thinking about it as we left the store and started walking down the block. He hadn't just winked at me, either, I remembered. He'd given me this really charming smile, too. The wink. The smile. The wink. The—

"Oh, Lucy." Mara put her hand on my arm. "I left my jacket back at the store. Would you run back and get it for me?"

The wink, the smile . . . the reality.

Cinderella does not get weekends off.

Chapter Five

Luckily, Ms. Daniels was done conferencing, so after I got my lunch Monday, I headed to the studio to eat it. On my way down the humanities corridor, I walked by Connor Pearson, who had his arm slung casually around Kathryn Ford. They looked like something out of a catalog advertising extremely beautiful teenagers. Just as I was trying to stop staring at him, Connor Pearson looked in my direction. Our eyes met and he studied me for a second, like he could almost but not quite remember who I was. Then he smiled a tremendous smile.

"*Heeey*—nice call on that Lakers game."

Instead of coming up with a witty response or just shrugging blithely, like I'm the kind of girl who's always getting compliments on her athletic acumen from hot senior guys, I totally froze. I just stood there, a deer in headlights.

Luckily my response (or lack thereof) didn't matter at all. Before even the wittiest person could possibly have tossed off the cleverest response, he was gone.

The art room was empty, but it didn't feel deserted. Handel's *Water Music* was playing on the tiny radio Ms. Daniels has on her desk, and the room's familiar smell of paint and turpentine and brewing coffee was all the company I needed. I flopped down on the paint-spattered sofa in the corner, pulled my sketch pad out of my bag, and idly flipped through the pages while nibbling the tasteless sandwich I'd just purchased. Was Ms. Daniels right? Was my art taking a direction? As I turned the pages, I tried to see my work as a stranger might, looking for patterns in the random sketches I'd drawn over the course of the past month. But as far as I could tell, everything looked more or less the same. I wanted to believe Ms. Daniels, that I was developing as an artist. But even calling myself an artist (albeit a developing one) seemed pretentious. I looked across the room at one of Sam Wolff's paintings. It was of a tree in winter—no leaves, dollops of wet snow dripping off branches. Like all of his work, it pulled you in, made you feel you were there, that if you touched the tree's bark, February's cold and damp would seep into your skin. Now, *he* was an artist. Unfortunately, he was also an antisocial jerk.

Was it possible for a person to have talent *and* a normal social life?

Maybe the real question was: Why am I, who has neither, fantasizing about having both?

When I got to the cafeteria on Friday, the sandwiches weren't out yet, which meant I had to stand alone waiting by the cash register for about ten years. I tried to cultivate a cool, disinterested demeanor, as if I were so above high school I didn't even know I attended one. *I'm actually deep in thought about extremely important intellectual trends. Even if you tried to approach me, I probably wouldn't respond.* When the cafeteria lady finally dumped a pile of sandwiches into the basket, I just grabbed one, not bothering to check its contents, threw some money in her direction, and raced toward the door.

I was halfway to freedom when I heard my name being called.

"Hello! Lucy Norton!" I looked around. Jessica Johnson and Madison Lawler were sitting at a table, waving frantically in my direction.

For a split second I considered pointing to myself and mouthing, "Who, me?" but considering that A) I am not a character in a sitcom, and B) they were both staring directly at me while Jessica yelled my full name, I chose instead to walk across the cafeteria to where they were sitting. As soon as I got to the table, Jessica grabbed my arm so hard her nails dug into my skin.

"Hey," I said. My greeting was casual in spite of

Jessica's clutching at me like I was the only thing standing between her and a lifesaving organ transplant.

"Can I just say that we thought you were *never* going to get here," said Jessica, pulling me toward her. She turned to Madison, who was nodding encouragingly. "Didn't I say, 'I'm totally going to start searching for her if she doesn't show up soon'?" Madison kept nodding, her ponytail following her head up and down, like punctuation.

"Oh," I said, though I considered asking, *Do you possibly have me confused with someone else?*

Madison expertly flicked a wisp of hair out of her face. Then she pointed at a chair across the table from her. "Sit."

I pulled out the chair and sat, waiting for my next command. *Bark! Roll over!* Jessica raised her eyebrows at me. "So," she said.

"So," I repeated.

"So," said Madison, "what fiery redhead who's new in the sophomore class has caught the eye of which—"

"Excuse me," said Jessica loudly, "I believe this is *my* little announcement." But Jessica didn't really seem to mind being interrupted. In fact, she smiled at Madison, and then both of them giggled. The whole thing was starting to make me very, very nervous. I squeezed my mystery sandwich, my hand sweaty against the Saran Wrap.

"Okay," said Jessica, taking a deep breath. "Who is the cutest guy in the entire school? Hint: he's a senior and he's on the basketball team."

Was this a trick question? Both Dave and Matt were seniors. I decided to stall for time.

"Well, that's kind of subjective," I said carefully.

While Madison made a face (either because of my stalling or because she didn't know what subjective meant), Jessica continued, "Does the name Connor Pearson mean anything to you?"

For a second I didn't say anything; I just opened and closed my mouth, like a fish. Then, as calmly as I could, I repeated, "Connor Pearson?"

Jessica leaned back without saying a word and raised her eyebrows, first at me and then at Madison. For a split second, I went cold with fear. Was this some elaborate, humiliating joke they'd concocted? I stayed silent, trying to re-create the set of circumstances that would have resulted in Madison and Jessica's deciding they wanted to take time out of their busy lives to torment me, but it was impossible. Let's face it: if Madison had the creative energy to come up with a scheme like the one I was imagining, she probably would have been in a more advanced math class.

"What about Connor Pearson?" I asked, keeping my voice even. Maybe this was simply some kind of Glen Lake High citizenship quiz. *What is our school mascot? How would you get from the science lab to the theater without going through the lobby? Who is the cutest senior in the school?*

Jessica shook her head, clearly bewildered by how difficult I was making this for everyone. Then she reached across the table and touched my hand, like maybe physical contact could penetrate my obtuseness. "How about *this* about Connor Pearson." She paused dramatically and squeezed my fingers. "Connor Pearson likes . . . drumroll, please . . ." She turned to make sure Madison was staring at her as intently as I was before turning back to me. "Lucy Norton."

A warm tingly sensation started in my head and proceeded to make its way down my body. Unlike most redheads, I don't have freckles and I don't blush—at least on the outside. But I could feel myself growing warmer; a trickle of sweat formed underneath my bra strap, and the sandwich almost slipped out of my hand.

Madison turned to Jessica. "She's speechless," she announced, grinning.

Jessica was grinning, too. "I told you she would be." She raised her eyebrows at Madison before turning back to me. "Connor told Dave to tell me to tell you that you should come to the game tonight. He said he thinks—" she paused to make eye contact with both of us, "you're cool."

My heart was pounding and something was suddenly wrong with my head, which seemed to be floating somewhere high above my body.

I cleared my throat. "Doesn't he, um, like, go out with Kathryn Ford?"

Jessica made a face as if I'd suggested Connor went out with Dave. "They're just friends," she said.

"Yeah," said Madison, waving my idea away like so much annoying cigarette smoke. "They're just friends."

We all sat there for a second, digesting this piece of information. Then Jessica touched my hand again and nodded enthusiastically. "So I say you should come to the game with us."

Madison's head bobbed up and down. "Yeah, Lucy. Come to the game tonight."

My brain was continuing to malfunction; I could see their lips move, but I could barely make out what they were saying. "Um, sorry, did you say tonight?" My mouth was so dry I had to peel my lips apart between words.

Jessica's smile turned to a grimace. "Whatever other plans you have, you *have* to cancel them."

Other plans? I almost laughed. When was the last time I'd had other plans?

Was this actually happening? Was I actually being invited to a basketball game by the hottest guy at Glen Lake? It was almost as if—

"Oh my god," I said out loud. Because all of a sudden, staring across the table at Madison, the truth hit me so hard I practically felt it smack me right between the eyes.

Prince Charming was requesting *my* presence tonight.

Jessica, misunderstanding my epiphany, shrieked, "I *know*!" Then she stretched her hands out, one toward Madison, the other toward me. "So are you coming?" she asked.

For a second I just sat there, staring across the table. With their matching suede jackets, artfully highlighted hair, and coordinated lipstick and eye liner, Madison and Jessica looked more like teen models than fairy godmothers. But there was no doubt that fairy godmothers were exactly what they were. Because you didn't have to be Walt Disney to see that my life *was* a fairy tale. And finally, after all this time, I'd arrived at the part where I got to live happily ever after.

I waited a minute, giving myself time to let the significance of what was happening sink in. Then I took a deep breath, laid my hand in Jessica's, and accepted my destiny.

"Definitely," I said.

Chapter Six

At five-thirty, just as I was finishing a second nervous breakdown and starting on my third, there was a knock on the basement door.

"Lucy, may I come down?" It was Mara.

"Yeah, sure." She came down the stairs holding a sample square of carpet in her hand, something I might have gotten excited about if she hadn't been coming downstairs with identical squares for the past six months. Who knew there were so many shades of beige on the planet?

"How's it going?" she asked.

"Okay," I said. It was a good thing she hadn't shown up five minutes before, when I was trying to stop my head from spinning by putting it between my knees and taking deep breaths.

She surveyed the floor, which was covered in clothes and books. "This room's a bit of a mess," she said.

"Yeah, sorry about that," I said.

Mara leaned against the wall, folding her arms across her chest. "I'd like to see you pick up after yourself a little more, Lucy."

I was tempted to ask the point of picking up after myself if I had no place to put *down* whatever I picked *up*. But that would have meant a whole discussion about how hard Mara was working to find just the right dresser and how much she wanted me to like my room and feel at home there once it was decorated. With less than an hour to shower, decide what to wear, get dressed, and have several more nervous breakdowns, this wasn't the time to explain to my stepmother that she didn't have to worry about my room feeling like home. We all know that after she meets the prince, Cinderella moves into the master bedroom suite of the royal palace. Once that happened, Mara could douse my dungeon with kerosene and strike a match.

Rather than try and explain my new circumstances, I decided to keep things simple. "I'll definitely clean up when I have a minute," I said. "I just can't do it right now."

"Do you have plans tonight?" Was it my imagination or did Mara sound shocked?

"Kind of," I said. Thinking about my plans, I started to get light-headed again; I hoped I wouldn't need to pant into a paper bag in front of my stepmother.

"Oh?"

"I kind of got invited to the game," I said. "By these girls I know."

"Who are the girls?" she asked, like she has the Glen Lake yearbook memorized and would immediately be able to recognize any one of the hundreds of girls I might have named.

"Um, they're just these girls I know," I said. Why is it I can spend a dozen Friday nights staring at the peeling walls of my "room" without anyone in the family so much as poking a head down to see if I'm still alive, while the one time I actually have plans (major plans, plans that necessitate extraordinary focus and massive preparation), my stepmother suddenly suggests we sing a duet of "Getting to Know You"?

I really wanted to ask Mara to give me some privacy, but I had to be careful about rejecting her motherly advances. If I do that, she gets all hurt, then she complains to my dad, and he gets mad at me for not giving her a chance. The most I could risk was turning my back to her ever so slightly as I started digging through a pile of clothes.

"How are you getting to the game?" Clearly Mara wasn't hip to the subtleties of body language.

"They're picking me up," I said, still not turning around.

There was a sharp intake of breath. "They drive? How old are they?"

"They're sophomores," I said, giving up and facing her. "They're picking me up in a cab."

Mara thought about what I'd said for a minute. "What time will you be home?"

I did a double take. *What time would I be home?* In San Francisco I'd never had an official curfew, I just had to call and let my dad know what time to expect me.

"I don't know," I said. "But I'll call if I'm going to be late."

"*Excuse* me?" said Mara. She said it like I'd just told her I'd call her from Charles de Gaulle if the evening went continental.

"I *said* I'll call if it gets late."

"Lucy, your father is not going to be happy when I tell him I have no idea what time to expect you home."

I clenched my teeth. Like I needed *her* to tell me under what circumstances my father would or would not be happy.

"Look, Mara, I don't know what to tell you. I won't be home too late." Remembering something Jessica had said to me at lunch, I added, "I think the guys have a curfew during the season or something."

Mara's eyes practically popped out of her head. Too late, I realized what I'd done. "The *guys*?" she said. "*What* guys?"

I forced myself to walk over to Mara and put my hand on her arm. We were in very, very delicate territory.

"I'm going to a basketball game with Jessica Johnson. You know, Jennifer's older sister?" Who would have guessed I'd be grateful to my stepsisters for their intimate knowledge of the J-J-J-Johnson family?

Mara nodded.

"Then we might get dinner after the game with some of the players," I added. "I'll be home by eleven." Really I had no idea what time I'd be home, but my dad's flight landed at six-thirty. By eleven I'd be dealing with him, not her.

"We-ell," she said. "Eleven sounds reasonable."

For a split second I was afraid I wouldn't be able to stop myself from screaming at her. *I don't have a curfew. The rule is I just have to call if I'm going to be late. I only said I'd be home by eleven to get you off my back, you evil, controlling witch.*

Luckily I was able to repress the urge to express these feelings. The only thing I couldn't control was how my hand tightened slightly on Mara's arm.

She confused my squeeze of rage with some kind of affectionate gesture and smiled at me. "I only want what's best for you," she said.

"Oh, I know, Mara."

I bet that's what Cinderella's stepmother said, too.

Standing in front of my bathroom mirror in a T-shirt and sweatpants, I could see that getting rid of Mara had catapulted me over one of the evening's many hurdles straight into another one: What was I going to wear?

My stepsisters' fashion advice echoed in my brain. *Lucy, you're not wearing* that *are you? Lucy, your pants are sooo five minutes ago. Ten minutes ago. Yesterday. Last month. Last year.*

Tonight I definitely did *not* want to look five minutes ago. I wanted to look now. I wanted to look cute. I wanted to look sexy. I wanted to look cool. The problem was, I had absolutely no idea what Glen Lake's standards *were* for hot, cute, sexy, or cool. At Wellington, everyone pretty much just wore jeans and T-shirts all the time. Even if there was a dance or something, people dressed as casually as possible, like they would never in a million years do something as lame as get dressed up for a school dance. I think the idea was to show up looking like you hadn't even known there *was* a dance; you'd just gone out to walk the dog or buy cigarettes or something, and the next thing you knew you were rockin' out with your classmates.

But people at Glen Lake dress up even for school. They wear *outfits*, color-coordinated shirts and pants and *socks*. I myself do not own any *outfits*. Unless you count jeans and a black T-shirt. Which is my totally five-minutes-ago uniform.

No way was I going to wear jeans and a black T-shirt to the game after wearing it basically every day of the year.

I finally decided to pair a tight, green scoop-neck

T-shirt with a little black skirt, black tights, and black boots with a low, chunky heel. Over the T-shirt, I put on an old Stanford sweatshirt of my dad's. I looked at myself in the mirror. It wasn't bad. The sweatshirt said, "I'm super caz," while the skirt said, "I'm super sexy."

Unless I was wrong and the whole ensemble simply said, "I'm super freaky." I stared at my reflection.

"Hey, Connor," I said nervously. My voice sounded high and tiny, Tropical Barbie pumped-up on estrogen.

I cleared my throat. "Hey, Connor," I said again, dropping my voice down an octave.

Now I sounded like Harvey Fierstein.

A car honked outside. My heart started pounding and I got a feeling in the pit of my stomach like I was about to throw up.

Another honk. I took a deep breath and exhaled, slowly.

"Hey, Connor," I said to the mirror. It sounded okay. Not perfect, but okay. I studied my reflection. Something still wasn't quite right. I took off the sweatshirt.

The car honked again.

I reached up and pulled out the ponytail holder. My hair fell around my face and shoulders, a wash of bright red.

I stared at myself, hard. With my hair down, I definitely didn't look like a female impersonator. And the green T-shirt looked good against the red. Not bad. Not bad at all.

I flipped off the light and raced upstairs.

"Sorry we're late," said Jessica, as she and Madison slid over to give me room next to them in the backseat. "This one here"—she pointed at Madison—"took about ten years deciding what to wear."

Madison shrugged and pointed at me. "I like your skirt," she said.

"Oh, thanks," I said, relieved.

"Hey, your little sisters are in my sister's class," said Jessica. "They're totally sweet."

The *Princesses? Sweet?*

"Uh, yeah," I said. "I guess Jennifer's their good friend." I managed not to add *for now* to the end of my sentence.

"Yeah, but she's a total brat," said Jessica. "She drives me crazy."

I knew there was a bonding opportunity presenting itself here, but I wasn't sure how to proceed. Did I say the Princesses were total brats, too, or would that make me look like a bitch? Maybe I was supposed to defend Jennifer, say she was sweet, like Jessica had said the Princesses were. As I analyzed and rejected half a dozen platitudes, I realized six months in social Siberia had taken their toll. I was no longer able to carry on even the most mundane conversation.

While I was busy trying to come up with a banal yet deeply significant observation about my monstrous stepsisters, the conversation moved on.

"Are you totally psyched about Connor?" asked Jessica.

"Well, I—"

"God, this color is way too dark," said Madison, who had taken a mirror out of Jessica's purse to check her lipstick.

It was true; her mouth was stained a disturbing shade of purple. She rubbed at her lips with a tissue.

Jessica took her hair out of its ponytail, turning toward me as she fluffed it around her face. "Wow," she said, "your hair is really red."

Was she making an observation or an accusation?

"Um, yeah," I said. My hand flew up to my head as if touching my hair would make it less red.

"I'm using your lip gloss," said Madison, reaching into Jessica's bag.

"Yeah, sure. Go ahead," said Jessica. She was still looking at me. "Is it natural?"

"Um, yeah," I said for the second time as Jessica took her bag back from Madison and dug around in it.

I should never have left my hair down. What had I been thinking? I felt utterly exposed, like I was living out the dream where you're walking down the hall in school and you suddenly realize you're not wearing any clothes. "My stepsisters keep telling me to dye it," I said, trying

to control my tone so it fell somewhere between statement and question. Was there a ponytail holder in my
bag?

"Why would you dye it?" asked Jessica, running her
brush through her hair. The look she gave me was one of
honest confusion. "It's totally hot."

"Oh, thanks," I said, forcing a laugh. "I mean, I
wasn't seriously thinking of dyeing it."

But, of course, for a second there, I had been.

I'd never been to a high-school basketball game before.
Officially, Wellington has a basketball team, but they're
not exactly state champion material, and no one I knew
ever followed their record too closely. Glen Lake's team,
on the other hand, is a juggernaut, something the bards
are expected to be singing of for the next hundred years.

As soon as we arrived I checked the score: 5–0, Glen
Lake. The visiting team was taking a free throw. I've
always loved watching players set up at the foul line. The
way they dribble slowly, stop, dribble again. They're like
religious figures working themselves into a mystical
trance. The guy making this shot was nervous, and he
held the ball for a long time before tossing it toward the
basket. Even before it left his hands you could tell it
wouldn't go in, but I watched it fall short of the net anyway, feeling the combination of sympathy and relief I
always feel when an opposing team misses a shot.

The gym, which could easily have held several

thousand people, was about two-thirds full, and the crowd was enthusiastic enough for twice as many people as were actually there. We climbed halfway up the crowded bleachers and sat down with a group of sophomores I didn't know. While Madison and Jessica talked to their friends, I looked down at the court and found Connor, who was yelling something to the guy who had the ball. Even from this distance he was beautiful. Unlike a lot of tall guys, he wasn't gangly and awkward, and his thick, dark hair fell just over his eyebrows. While I was watching, he shook it out of his face and then ran his hand through it. I felt a little jolt of electricity tingle in my own hand.

The score quickly got crazy close. In the fourth quarter Glen Lake had a short run of making one basket after another, but then the other team caught up and we were tied for a long time. I was on the edge of my seat, especially at this one really tense moment when Connor and the team's shooting guard headed toward the basket like there was nothing that would stop them from scoring. They passed the ball easily back and forth until the shooting guard, suddenly surrounded, tried, and failed to get around the guys who were guarding him. I held my breath while he dribbled in place, looking for an opening, then passed to the center, who, in a nearly impossible shot from just outside the three-point circle, sank the ball. I pumped my fist in the air and screamed, "YES!"

"What?" asked Jessica, who'd been talking to Madison.

"You *missed* that?" I asked. Our whole side was cheering. Even though we were sitting right next to each other, I had to shout to be heard.

"What?" she asked, "What did I miss?" and suddenly Madison was staring at me, too.

"Number seventeen just scored," I explained. "We're up by two." I wondered if the reason they weren't exactly watching the game had something to do with the fact that Matt and Dave had yet to get off the bench.

"Oh my god, that's Matt's brother," said Madison, slapping her cheeks with her hands so that she looked like *The Scream*. "I can't believe I missed it."

"Nice you," said Jessica. "Better hope Matt doesn't ask about it."

Madison flipped her hair out of her face. "Puh-leeze," she said. "What's he going to do, grill me about the game?" Then she laughed. "And if he does, Lucy can help me. Right Lucy?" She dropped her arm around my shoulders and gave me a squeeze, pressing her cheek into my back for a second before letting go.

"Right," I said.

When Connor sank the final winning basket, even Jessica and Madison were on their feet. The wave of pleasure that washed over me was something way more intense than any kind of school spirit. All over the bleachers people were calling Connor's name. He smiled up at the fans and even gave a little wave, which just made people yell louder. I knew he hadn't been waving at *me*, but still. *Connor Pearson knows who I am*, I found myself thinking. *He knows my name.* Of course, my name was just about the only thing he *did* know about me, but it was something.

After all, what did Prince Charming know about Cinderella besides her shoe size?

Chapter Seven

Piazzolla's is in the village of Glen Lake in an old wooden structure that used to be a working mill and sits right on the river that runs through the center of town. It's actually a cool-looking building, unlike the rest of Glen Lake, which has this whole faux "ye olde towne of Glenne Loch" thing going. If you saw Piazzolla's from the outside you might think it's a fancy Italian restaurant because it's all dark wood and dim lighting, but basically it's just a pizza place. When we got inside, there was a long line made up almost entirely of people who had been at the game.

Jessica, Madison, and I had taken a cab over from school, and by the time Dave, Matt, and Connor arrived, hair wet from the showers, there was only one group ahead of us waiting for a table. Personally, I wouldn't have minded if there were fifty groups ahead of us, since

I was a nervous wreck. How was I possibly going to swallow even a single bite of pizza? I was on a date. I was on a date with the most popular guy in school. I was on a date with the most popular guy in school and *I had never been on a date in my life.*

My anxiety wasn't exactly assuaged by the fact that as soon as the guys walked in, the two couples started making out while Connor and I just stood there. His wet hair was shiny, and his cheeks were flushed.

"Hey," he said, smiling. "You made it."

"I made it," I said. His eyes were impossibly blue, and as we looked at each other, he put his hand on my shoulder, leaned in, and just barely grazed my cheek with his lips. I got the faintest whiff of something musky and delicious—cologne or soap or shampoo, I wasn't sure. My heart leaped into my throat and I couldn't catch my breath. I was positive I was going to pass out.

Luckily right then the couples stopped kissing and Connor took a step back.

"Dave, Matt, you know Lucy," said Jessica.

"Hey," said Dave.

"Hey," said Matt.

"Hey," I said. "Great game."

Matt and Dave both grunted their thanks; I wondered if they felt weird taking credit for a victory they'd had nothing to do with. Then again, maybe they were just bitter about Chicago losing to the Lakers last week. As I was trying to decide how I could broach the subject of the Bulls without sounding like I was gloating, the hostess came over to where we were standing and called Jessica's name.

"That's us," said Jessica. "Table for six."

As we snaked through the restaurant behind the hostess, Connor draped his arm casually over my shoulder, like it was something he'd done a million times before. We passed at least four or five tables of Glen Lake students, and at each one someone waved and said, "Hey, Connor" or "Great game, Connor" or "How's it going, Connor?" and even, simply, "C-*dawg*!" Connor didn't stop to talk to anyone, but he smiled a lot and said, "Hey, man," a few times to people I didn't know. Everyone who called out to Connor smiled at me, which was pretty cool, even if some of the smiles felt like little question marks.

As soon as the waiter took our orders, Madison turned to Connor. "That was an incredible shot," she said. I wondered if she had actually seen him sink the winning basket, or if she was just repeating what she'd heard other people say.

"Yeah," said Dave. "Nice going." He and Connor high-fived across the table.

"Thanks, man," said Connor. He'd taken off his jacket and his sweater and was just wearing a snug gray T-shirt that showed how well defined his shoulders were. My stomach flipped over, and I had to look away.

"So, Red," he said. It took a minute before I realized

he was talking to me. "How'd you like the game?" He put his hand on the back of my chair.

"It was a great game," I told him. "I was biting my nails the whole time."

"Lucy knows everything about basketball," Jessica informed Connor.

"Well, after that Lakers' victory, I'm planning to take her predictions a lot more seriously," said Connor, smiling a private smile at me.

"What?" asked Madison, and when Connor didn't explain, she turned to Matt. "What predictions?" she asked.

I smiled back at Connor and looked into his blue, blue eyes. "Is that why you wanted me to come tonight?" I asked, tilting my head. "To get my picks for the finals?"

He arched an eyebrow at me. "Maybe it is," he said. "Maybe it is."

When there was nothing left of the two large pies we'd ordered except a few pieces of crust, Jessica, Madison, and I excused ourselves and went to the bathroom. While Jessica and I peed, Madison stood in front of the mirror telling us how many calories are in a slice. As soon as I came out of the stall, Madison turned to me and asked if I thought she looked fat. When I said no, she waited for Jessica to emerge and then asked if *she* thought she looked fat. Jessica said no. Madison said we were both lying and pinched the flesh just above her hip to prove it.

When we got back to the table, there was a pile of money in the center. I reached into my bag for some cash.

"Don't worry about it," said Connor, "I've got you."

I've got you.

Then he smiled at me, like paying for my dinner was the most natural thing in the world.

"Thanks," I said. But what I meant was, Connor, you *have* got me.

Connor stood up and so did Dave and Matt. "You ladies can treat us to ice cream," said Matt.

"Ah, hello," said Madison as we followed the guys out of Piazzolla's, "I am so not eating ice cream. Do you know how many grams of fat are in an ice-cream cone?"

We walked down Main Street toward a gelato place, and for the first block or two I felt totally self-conscious about how silent Connor and I were being. Jessica and Dave were having some kind of heated conversation (Jessica was waving her arms around and Dave kept nodding), and Madison and Matt were laughing, but Connor and I were just walking along not talking at all. Right when I was sure my lack of having anything interesting to say was turning my dream date into a nightmare, Connor took his hand and put it on the back of my neck.

You might think it's uncomfortable to have someone hold you by the neck, but it isn't. Quite the opposite, in fact. I don't know if it was all that practice with a basketball, but Connor Pearson knew just how to put his hand on the back of someone's neck—not too gently, not too tightly. By the time we got to the gelato place, he was using his thumb and forefinger to give me a really light massage, and I knew it didn't matter that we weren't talking.

We wandered around the village eating our ice cream for a while until the guys had to get home for curfew. Madison waved at me as she and Matt walked over to his car, and Jessica gave me a hug as passionate as any of the post-math ones she exchanges with Madison.

"I'll see you Monday," she called, finally releasing me and heading off to Dave's car.

"Yeah, see you Monday," I said. Connor and I walked to his car and he held the door open while I slid onto the cool leather seat.

All night I'd been trying to maintain my air of sophisticated nonchalance, like going out with cute, popular, older guys was something I'd done fairly regularly at Wellington. Now that Connor and I were alone together, however, the facade was cracking. Violently. My stomach was in knots. My mouth was Saharan. I reached into my bag to get out a mint. But as soon as my fingers made contact with the tin, it occurred to me that perhaps popping a curiously strong breath mint right as I got in the car would seem slutty, like, *Hello, I assume we'll be making out momentarily, and I'd like to be pre-*

pared. I zipped my bag shut leaving the Altoids inside.

I'd never been in a car with a guy before. I mean, obviously I'd been in a car with a male member of the species, but I had never been driven home *from* a date *by* a date. Connor hit a button on the radio and Mos Def came on. The volume was a little too loud for us to talk, but Connor didn't seem to mind, so neither did I. He rested his hand lightly on my knee as he drove.

When we got to my neighborhood, I spoke my first and only words of the entire ride: "Make a left at the corner," followed by "It's the third one on the right."

"Well, this is it," I said. As Connor pulled up in front of my house and put the car in park, my duplicitous palms started sweating.

"Hey, Red," he said, and he unbuckled his seat belt.

In the dim light from the dashboard, I could just make out his chiseled cheekbones and perfect profile. And then everything began to get blurry, and I realized he was leaning toward me.

His lips were soft, and he put his hands on either side of my neck and moved his fingers gently through my hair. Kissing him felt like drinking a glass of cold, clear water when you're parched. I wanted it to go on forever. When he finally pulled away and I opened my eyes, I couldn't really focus them.

"I should go," he said softly. "Curfew."

"Oh, right," I said. "Curfew."

"I had a great time tonight," he said.

I could barely form words; my lips were made of liquid.

"Me, too," I finally managed to say.

"So I'll see you Monday?" he said.

I nodded, reached over to open the door, and started to get out without taking off my seat belt, which jerked me back. I landed right where I'd started.

"I forgot to take off my seat belt," I said. Even though I hadn't had anything to drink, I felt drunk.

"Yeah," he said, and he leaned in and kissed me again before reaching down to unbuckle my seat belt for me. "There you go," he said.

"Thanks," I said. I slid out the door and shut it behind me. Now it was as if my entire body had turned to water; it took some focus for me to coordinate stepping away from the car.

I turned and watched as Connor drove off. My cheeks felt hot and my lips swollen, as if I'd been biting them. Then I floated up to the house, realizing it was possible I had just experienced the most perfect night of my life.

Apparently being Cinderella isn't so bad after all.

Chapter Eight

When I woke up in the morning I felt as good as if *I'd* won the NBA finals. Not only had I had the most perfect, amazing, incredible (not to mention *only*) date of my life, I was actually about to spend the day alone with my dad, something that hadn't happened since we'd lived on a different coast.

"Lucy, you up?" It was my dad yelling down from the kitchen. I looked at the clock—ten-fifteen. We were supposed to be on our way to the Guggenheim in thirty minutes.

"I'm up!" I yelled, throwing the covers off myself and leaping out of bed. My dad *hates* waiting for people.

As I rushed to get ready, I kept the movie of kissing Connor running in my mind. I saw him lean toward me, perfectly backlit by the streetlight. I felt his hand on my waist, his lips brushing up against my temple.

Usually my dad starts pacing around the room like a caged animal, checking his watch and sighing dramatically as ETD approaches. But this morning when I came upstairs, he was calmly reading the paper in the living room, and I was the one who was antsy to leave. I couldn't wait to get in the car and start telling him all about my night.

Well, maybe not *all* about it.

"Chop-chop, Mister," I said, pointing at my wrist where my watch, if I wore one, would have been. "You think Patton read the Arts and Leisure section on D-Day?"

My dad looked up. "Well, well, well, aren't we timely," he said. "You look practically ready to walk out the door."

"And you can drop the 'practically.' I'm walkin'." I started toward the door.

"I think Mara's running a little late," my dad said. "We're adjusting ETD by half an hour."

"Mara?" I said it like I'd never heard the name before.

"Don't worry, Sergeant, we'll have her up to our punctuality standards soon," said my dad.

I was glad my back was to him so he couldn't see the expression on my face. I tried to make my voice neutral. "I just didn't . . . I mean I didn't realize she was coming," I said. Once I'd managed to work my mouth into some semblance of a smile, I turned around.

"Sure, she's coming," said my dad. He looked confused. "Why wouldn't she come?"

Well, why would she? "I thought we were, you know, going into the city just the two of us." I tried to remember the actual conversation in which I'd told him about the exhibit. Had he mentioned Mara's coming? When I said "together" did he think I meant the *three* of us together?

Now my dad was frowning. He lowered his voice. "Lucy, I think it would really hurt Mara's feelings if she thought you didn't *want* her to come with us."

I lowered mine, too. "It's not that I don't want her to come," I began. But then I didn't know how to finish the sentence. Because quite frankly, that's *exactly* what it was.

"I thought you liked Mara," said my dad. He didn't seem mad anymore, he seemed hurt, like I'd opened a present he'd been really excited to give me only to see my face fall.

"I *do* like Mara," I said. "Really." I went over to where he was sitting and dropped to the floor by the side of his chair. He put his hand on my head.

"Honey, we're a family now," he said. "And families do things together."

I was about to say that plenty of the families I know do things separately, but just as I opened my mouth, Mara came down the stairs.

"Ta-da!" she said, standing in the archway between

the living room and the foyer. "Only fifteen minutes late. A personal best."

My dad applauded. "And worth every extra second," he said. She came over and kissed the top of his head, then bent down and kissed the top of mine. My scalp tingled with annoyance where her lips had touched it.

"Ready?" she asked.

"You betcha," said my dad, standing. He stretched out his hand to help me up from the floor. "Lucy? You ready?"

I looked up. His face was a mixture of concern and impatience I'd never seen before. "Yeah," I said, reaching my hand up to take his. "I'm ready."

When we got to the car, I opened the passenger-side door and was about to get in when I saw my dad looking at me. He frowned and shook his head slightly.

I made a face at him and gestured toward the seat. "Hop in," I said to Mara.

"Now, that's what I call service," she said, slipping into the car. I shut the door and opened the one behind it, sliding across the backseat to sit in the middle. I caught my dad's eye as he looked into the rearview mirror before backing up.

"You okay back there?" he asked.

But it was more of a statement than a question, so I gave the answer I knew he wanted. "Sure," I said. "Just great."

"That's what we like to hear," he said, putting the car in reverse.

It certainly is, I thought. It certainly is.

"Thanks to Lucy, we're seeing one of the hottest art shows in New York," my dad said, reaching across the gearshift and taking Mara's hand. There was no traffic on the parkway, and he was driving about a thousand miles an hour. "Clemente's huge right now." Lying across the backseat, I rolled my eyes at the roof of the car.

Mara turned around and smiled at me. "How did you hear about the show?"

I knew she was only talking to me because my dad was there, so I kept my answer as brief as possible. "From my art teacher."

Mara was still turned around facing me. "It must be nice for you to have a teacher you respect so much for art class," said Mara.

"Yeah? Why's that?"

Mara's always going on about how important it is that girls have good teachers for math and science because once they hit high school, they apparently start flunking those subjects. It's pretty funny to hear her go off on her feminist tirades, considering she's spent her entire adult life being supported by not just one but *two* husbands. I think my stepmother's idea of equal opportunity is women taking every chance they can to charge something to a man's credit card.

She dropped my dad's hand, reached behind her, and patted my thigh before turning to face forward again. "Well, I guess I was thinking how important Ms. Daniels must be since your mom was an artist," she said.

Mara's totally convinced I never talk about my mom because of how traumatized I was by her death. It's one of the many brilliant theories of human behavior she's concocted from the library of self-help books she accumulated during her years as a divorcée. I sat up and tried to get my dad to make eye contact with me by staring in the rearview mirror, but in spite of its being an overcast day, he had put on his Terminator sunglasses, and I couldn't find his eyes.

"She's okay," I said, and I lay back down again.

The Guggenheim Museum is at the corner of Fifth Avenue and Eighty-Ninth Street, directly across from Central Park. Frank Lloyd Wright designed the strange and beautiful building—a stack of white circles that expands from the bottom up. Today the museum was packed with tourists, most of whom looked like they'd just stepped off a cruise ship and couldn't wait to reboard. As we stood reading the exhibit's introductory panel, Mara, who was leaning up against my dad, whispered something in his ear, and he laughed and wrapped the arm that wasn't around her waist across her chest.

Was this what he meant by families doing things together?

"Hey, Dad, check it out," I said, "wouldn't that be a great name for a band—Prodigious Oeuvre?" I pointed at the phrase on the panel.

My dad had been whispering something into Mara's ear when I started talking, and now they both looked at me, like they'd forgotten I was even there.

"What'd you say, honey?" he asked.

Just as I was about to repeat myself, my dad tickled Mara, who let out a yelp and said, "Doug!"

God, compared to the two of them, Madison and Matt actually had a sense of decorum.

"I said I think I'm going to go on ahead," I said.

"How come?" Mara had her fingers intertwined with my dad's. Her cheeks were flushed.

"I kind of have to look at some things for class."

"You mean like an assignment?" asked my dad. He ran a hand through Mara's hair, letting the fingers rest at the nape of her neck. I thought of last night and Connor holding my neck.

Everything had officially gotten just a little too weird.

"Yeah, exactly," I lied. "Like an assignment."

"Well, okay," he said. "I guess we'll find each other at the end."

I was already stepping back, letting myself get lost in the crowd. "Great," I said, nodding enthusiastically. "I'll see you at the end."

I made my way past decades of Clemente's work,

too mad to see any of the brightly colored canvases surrounding me. If all he was going to do was nuzzle Mara, why had my dad even bothered to come? Had he actually *wanted* to ruin my day? That was a plausible theory, except that in order to plan on ruining my day, my dad would have actually had to think about me, something he clearly never did anymore.

And then, suddenly, just as I was considering storming out onto Fifth Avenue and putting Mara, my dad, and the museum behind me, I was stopped in my tracks by a painting that took up almost an entire wall: a crazed face of red and green and yellow. The mouth was open in a grimace, and each tooth was a skull. The tongue was an impossibly pale, delicate pink. Sitting on the razor's edge of the beautiful and the grotesque, it was unlike any work of art I'd ever seen.

I don't know how long I'd been standing there, gaping, when I noticed the guy who kept looking back and forth from the painting to me. I stood up a little straighter before I realized it was just Sam Wolff from my art class. Sam's got black, curly hair, and when he's painting or drawing, he pulls on it, so usually when I see him his hair's standing more or less straight up from his head. But I guess when he hasn't been doing that, it lies a lot flatter, which would explain my failure to recognize him at first.

"Hey," he said, turning to face me. "You're in my art class." He didn't smile.

"Oh, right," I said. "I was trying to figure out where I know you from. What are you doing here?" I wondered if Ms. Daniels had told him to come to the museum, too. On the one hand, I liked the idea that I was the only student she'd told about the exhibit. On the other, if she was going to lump me with another one of her students, Sam Wolff wasn't exactly shabby artistic company.

"What am I *doing* here?" asked Sam. He looked around at the paintings and then back at me. "I'm shopping for a sofa bed."

I couldn't tell if he was laughing with me or at me. "Funny," I said.

When he didn't say anything, I should probably have taken his silence as a subtle sign that he was *not interested in pursuing a conversation*, yet I plunged on. "So, do you like the exhibit?" I asked.

He'd gone back to looking at the painting. "What?" he asked distractedly.

"Do you like the exhibit?" My question, which hadn't exactly been brilliant the first time around, sounded utterly inane the second.

"Do I *like* it?" Sam repeated my question slowly, rolling the syllables around in his mouth either because he wasn't sure how to answer it or because he felt he was tasting a new and particularly impressive flavor of idiocy.

"Yes," I repeated in a snotty voice. "Do you *like* it?" Why was I being so rude? After all, he'd just repeated my question. Lots of people did that and I didn't snap at them. But there was something about the way he was standing there, silently, like he was all alone with the painting, like I wasn't even there, that was driving me crazy.

Then again that was kind of how I'd been standing there a minute ago.

Sam finally looked at me. "Yes," he said. "I like it."

"Oh," I said, unprepared for such a civil response. "Well, I like it, too."

Sam ran his hand through his hair. With his curls once again veering straight up to the ceiling, he looked more like the guy in my art class than he had a minute ago.

"That's . . . great," he said.

"Yeah," I said. "Great."

He glanced down at his watch. "Well, I gotta go," he said. "I'm meeting someone downtown."

"Oh, yeah, of course," I said. I looked at my watchless wrist. "I should get going soon, too."

"Okay. Well, bye," he said, turning to go.

"Yeah, okay. Bye." I watched him disappear into the crowd.

I wandered into a little room off the main exhibition space. In the past, whenever my dad and I went to a museum, we played this game where we each had to pick which painting we'd want if we could have only one. I tried to play the game by myself, walking slowly through the room and pausing before each piece as I imagined owning it. The stuff here was completely different from the painting I'd just been looking at; everything in this room was either a page from a tiny illuminated manuscript or an equally intricate pencil drawing. I imagined hanging first one piece and then another in my room. But it wasn't any fun without having someone to show what I'd picked, so finally I quit trying and headed back down to the lobby. I ended up wandering into the gift shop, where my dad and Mara were comparing napkin rings. I watched them for a minute, laughing and talking together, before I called out to my dad. He looked up, but he didn't seem especially glad to see me or anything.

The whole ride back in the car, I tried to figure out what was wrong with me. How can you be Cinderella *after* she meets the prince and still feel so incredibly sad?

Chapter Nine

The first thing I did when the bus pulled up to school on Monday morning was check to see if Connor's SUV was in the senior parking lot. Which it was. I'll say this for the car-dependent suburbs—it's much easier to track a crush here than in a major metropolitan area like San Francisco.

On the way to chemistry, my last class before lunch, I still hadn't seen Madison, Jessica, or Connor, but I was starting to get a really weird feeling. Everywhere I went small groups of people were whispering to each other. At first I wondered if some scandal had taken place over the weekend, like back in November when two kids got expelled for selling Ecstasy. On my way from chemistry to the cafeteria, though, I started to sense the buzz was more localized, something that followed me around. Two conversations ended just as I walked by and started up again as soon as I was out of earshot. I thought I was being paranoid, but then I passed a group of senior girls I didn't know talking by their lockers. As soon as I was within hearing distance they stopped talking and watched me. Then, as I walked by, they said, "Hey," even though I'd never spoken a word to any of them.

"Hey," I said back, thinking, *What's the deal?*

Suddenly I started to get a bad feeling in my stomach. What if Connor had told Dave or Matt about how we'd made out in the car, only he'd turned it into some kind of joke. *Yeah, man, she was so into me. She practically lost her friggin' mind when I kissed her.* I remembered how I'd been so disoriented I'd tried to get out of the car without taking off my seat belt. Could that be what everyone was whispering about? Remembering all the movies I'd ever seen where the cute, popular guy asks out the ugly, unpopular girl on a dare, I walked faster, not meeting the eyes of anyone I passed.

The cafeteria was crowded, but instead of taking my sandwich and heading for the exit and the studio, I found myself walking toward the table where Madison and Jessica and I had sat on Friday. As I got closer, I could see Jessica sitting there alone, but just as I was about to wave, I stopped myself. What if she and Madison *had* concocted this whole setup with Connor in order to humiliate me? Why had I been so quick to dismiss Madison as too stupid to come up with a complex practical joke? This was what happened when you underestimated people—they destroyed you.

I decided I'd slow down as I approached Jessica's table but wouldn't stop. That way if she didn't ask me to sit with her, I could pretend I was just passing by on my way to join all of my other friends. When I was two tables away, I cut my speed in half, and by the time I was one table from Jessica's, a paralytic snail could have overtaken me. Just as I was about to start walking in place, Jessica looked up, saw me, and squawked with delight.

"Oh my god," she said, running over and giving me a hug. "Can I just say," she walked me back to the table and pulled me down next to her, "that you two are adorable together?"

"You really think so?" I felt the urge to administer a polygraph test right there on the spot.

"Oh my god, are you kidding? I wish you could have seen yourselves. It's all we talked about all weekend. We wanted to call you, but we don't know your cell. So we just kept going, 'Don't they make the cutest couple?'"

I didn't know what to say. I'd never been part of a cute couple before.

"Hel-*lo*!" Madison called, walking toward us. She collapsed into the chair opposite Jessica's with her enormous backpack on her lap. "Please tell me one of you knows something about imagery in *The Great Gatsby*."

"We read that first semester. It's all about the green

light," said Jessica. "Just keep talking green light."

"For *five typed pages*?" Madison shook her head and changed the subject. "But enough about me. How are you guys?"

My spokesperson responded with alacrity. "How do you *think* she is?" She put her arm around my shoulders and gave me a hug. "She's only, like, Connor Pearson's girlfriend."

"I know!" Madison practically shouted. She pushed her backpack to the floor and leaned toward me. "He's totally into you. He told Matt he thought you were really smart." She paused and smiled at me. "And really sexy. He said he's going to ask you to come to the game on Friday." She took my hand in hers and then reached out for Jessica's, too. "How incredibly cool is this?"

"Okay, tell us *everything*," said Jessica. She was smiling and squeezing my hand tightly.

When was the last time anyone had wanted me to tell her *anything*, much less everything? Their curiosity was the warmth of the sun after a swim in the frigid ocean.

"Is he a good kisser?" asked Madison.

"Yeah," I admitted. "He's a good kisser."

Jessica and Madison each gave my hand a squeeze. "We knew it!" Madison said.

"So, wait," said Jessica. "How good?"

I couldn't help smiling at the memory of kissing Connor.

"Oooh, she's smiling," said Madison.

I took my hands back and dropped my face into them. "Stop," I said through my fingers. "You're embarrassing me."

"Okay, we'll stop," said Jessica. But when I looked up she and Madison were still staring and smiling at me.

"You are, like, so cool," Jessica announced, and Madison nodded as if Jessica had just recited a holy truth.

Looking at their awestruck faces, I could literally see the power of Connor's touch. With his kiss, the prince had turned this unlovable stepdaughter into a popular girl.

I didn't run into Connor until after sixth period, when we were coming toward each other from opposite ends of the hallway. I saw him before he saw me, and watching him from a distance, I remembered all the times I'd passed him in the hall before today, totally aware of who he was while he didn't even know I existed. Then he spotted me, and suddenly he was smiling from ear to ear, like seeing me was the greatest thing that had happened to him all day.

Was he really my boyfriend now? It didn't seem possible.

"Hey, Red," he called, slowing down. He was wearing a soft-looking green sweater with his basketball jacket over it. The hall swarmed with people going to class, and out of the corner of my eye, I noticed some of them checking us out.

"Hey, Connor," I said. A girl I didn't know walked by and said, "Hi, Connor," and he waved in her direction without looking up.

"So you're coming to the game Friday, right?"

"Right," I said. Thinking about the game and then going out with him after made me feel all tingly, and I shivered a little.

"Are you cold?" he asked.

"Oh, no, I'm just—"

But he was already slipping his jacket off and draping it over my shoulders. It was heavy and smelled of whatever delicious soap or cologne or shampoo Connor used.

"Hey, you look pretty good in that," he said, admiring me. "Why don't you keep it for a while?" He took my hand for a second.

"Yeah, sure," I said. "I'll keep it for a while." I felt faint. I actually felt faint. And I knew that if I fainted, Connor would pick me up in his arms and carry me to the nurse's office, and the image of him doing that only made me feel fainter. Luckily, just then the warning bell sounded. "Gotta go," he said. "Higby'll go nuts if I'm late." And he turned and was swallowed up by the crowd.

By the time I got to English, my last class of the day, I must have said hi to at least fifty people. Maybe a hundred and fifty. It was like I was a celebrity or something. As I walked into the empty classroom, I realized it was the first time I'd been alone since lunch. I sat down in my usual seat, opened my notebook to a blank page, and started doodling, glad to have the quiet room to myself. My solitude, however, was to be short lived. A minute later Rachel Smith came into the room and rushed over to where I was sitting, pulling out the chair of the desk next to mine.

As she sat down, she blew a massive bubble in my direction. "I saw you at Piazzolla's Friday," she said.

"Oh, yeah," I said. "I had dinner there." Was that what we'd done at Piazzolla's? I couldn't actually remember eating a thing.

"Want some gum?" she held out a pack in my direction. Through the wrapping I got a whiff of something very strawberry.

"No thanks," I said.

She put the gum back in her bag. "I waved as you were leaving, but I guess you didn't see me."

She'd waved at me? "I guess not," I said. "Sorry." Just then Bethany Miller came in and made a beeline for the empty desk on my other side.

"Hey," said Bethany. She was wearing a miniskirt that would have been too small on a house cat. When she took off her jacket, her boobs practically fell out of her low-cut shirt and onto her desk. She gave me an enormous smile.

"Hey," I said. Rachel and Bethany, who were best friends, usually sat right next to each other so they could pass notes from the second class started to the second it ended. Once, in September, I made the mistake of sitting at the empty desk next to Bethany's, and she asked me to move. Actually, she didn't *ask* me to move, she *told* me to move. What she said was, "You're sitting in my friend's seat."

"You and Connor Pearson are the *cutest* couple," Bethany squealed. "You guys looked so good together Friday." She squeezed my shoulder when she said "Friday." Then she dropped her hand onto my desk.

"Um, thanks."

"'Cause you're both, like, tall and thin and stuff. You look like two models."

"Thanks," I said again. If there's one thing I know I don't look like, it's a model. I looked down at my doodle as the rest of the class started filing in. A few people smiled at me or said hey.

"Oooh, that's cool," said Rachel, looking at my notebook. "It really looks like a glass of water."

Bethany looked down to admire my drawing, too. "Totally. Are you, like, a really good artist? Because that's really good." She nodded enthusiastically, then repeated. "Really."

"Oh, I'm not—" I started to say, but just then Miss Merriam walked in.

"Let's settle down, class," she said.

Rachel reached over and tapped my shoulder. Then she mouthed, "Call me."

I nodded, too surprised to mention I didn't have her number.

I may have become royalty at school, but my elevated status didn't have any effect on my home life, where I remained invisible as ever. At dinner Mara and her daughters talked exclusively about the shopping spree they'd gone on after school (without me, naturally). Princess One couldn't decide if she should have gotten a sweater in green, like Princess Two had, or if she was right to have gotten it in blue, like Mara had. Mara promised they could go back to the mall on Friday and Princess One could get the green sweater, too.

While Princess Two complained about how unfair that was, Mara listened intently, taking tiny bites of her food and following each with a sip of water.

"Oh, girls, I almost forgot," she said after assuring Princess Two she could get another sweater also. "Your father called and said you need to bring something nice to wear this weekend because they're having people for dinner on Saturday night."

"I *hate* when they have company," whined Princess One, clacking her fork against her plate for emphasis.

"It's *so* unfair," said Princess Two. "We have to sit there and not say anything and everyone ignores us."

"I'm going to speak to Diana about that," said

Mara. "The two of you are a lovely addition to any dinner party. She should be more gracious."

The Princesses hate their stepmother Diana with a passion, and I got the sense the feeling was mutual. I'd met Diana a couple of times when she and the Princesses' dad dropped them off or picked them up, and I always tried to use ESP to let her know I shared her feelings and supported her one hundred percent.

"I'm sorry, sweetheart," said Mara. I swear, she was practically tearing up. It was all I could do not to puke up my risotto.

"You don't understand," said Princess Two. Then she slumped down in her seat like going to her father's was the equivalent of going to the electric chair. "You don't know what it's like to live with Diana."

I wanted to point out that actually *she* doesn't know what it's like to live with Diana considering she "lives" with her about four days out of every thirty. Then I wanted to point out that *I'm* the one who lives with her horrible stepmother three hundred and sixty-five days a year, and that if I only had to do it two weekends a month, I'd consider myself lucky.

I finished my risotto and spooned some more onto my plate. Mara watched what I was doing with her eyebrows raised. "Lucy, you don't need to gobble your food. It's not going anywhere."

"Sorry."

"If you eat too fast, your brain can't register that

your stomach is full. That's why you should take tiny bites and wash each one down with a sip of water."

Just as I was about to tell Mara what she could do with her water, the phone rang. I looked at my watch. Eight o'clock. The only hope I had of getting even a second alone on the phone with my dad was if I moved faster than Mara. "I'll get it," I said. I raced into the kitchen with my plate and grabbed the phone.

"Hey, Dad," I said, still holding my plate.

"Hey, Goose," he said. "How's it going?"

"Okay," I said. I wanted to tell him just how okay things really were, since usually my okay was a total lie, but there was no time for that. Through the open door, I saw Mara stand and make her way toward the phone in the den.

"Are you going to watch any of the Knicks game?" he asked. The other line rang, and I heard Mara pick up. I hoped it was one of her friends calling about a new home-decorating scheme, something guaranteed to keep my stepmother occupied for hours.

"Maybe," I said. "Probably just the fourth quarter, though." I rinsed my plate off and slipped it into the dishwasher. The thing about a Knicks game is you know how it's going to end—defeat. Still, every once in a while they can surprise you.

There was a click. "Lucy?" God, couldn't she leave us alone for two minutes?

"Yeah?"

"Phone's for you."

"For me?" I couldn't imagine who it would be. Neither Jessica nor Madison had said anything about calling me later.

"Bye," said my dad.

"Bye, Dad," I said. I heard him say "Hello, darling," before I had a chance to hang up.

I pushed the button for our second line. "Hello?"

"Hey, Red."

My heart started pounding. I squeezed my hand into a fist and pressed it against my scalp, hoping the pressure would somehow keep me from floating into outer space. "Hey," I said.

"How's it going?"

"Okay," I said. "How's it going with you?"

"Not too bad," he said. There was a pause. This was definitely not good. It's one thing to have a long silence when you're walking next to someone and he's massaging your neck. It's another to be on the phone with that someone and have nothing to say.

I wracked my brain for a conversation starter. "You watching the game?" I asked finally.

"You know it. In fact, you hear that?" I could hear something in the background, but I couldn't tell what it was. Luckily, Connor answered his own question. "That's Madison Square Garden in surround sound."

"Not too shabby," I said. "But won't those great acoustics make it all the more depressing when they lose?"

"Ouch, woman. You're harsh." I could tell from his voice that he was smiling, and I smiled, too. I slid down the wall until I was sitting on the floor.

"Well, if the shoe fits," I said.

"Listen, you," he said. "Just because you're cute, don't think you can get away with dissing the home team."

Connor Pearson had just told me I was cute. I bit down on the telephone cord to keep from screaming.

In the background, I heard the announcer say something.

"All right, I'm gonna go watch, Red. I'll call you at halftime, okay?"

"Okay," I said. Connor hung up, but I waited a minute before standing and putting the receiver back in the cradle. I could see from the light that Mara and my dad were still talking on line one. Normally I might have gotten annoyed, but tonight I didn't care. Let them talk until dawn if they wanted.

I had a game to watch.

Chapter Ten

I would have said that nothing could make me not like Ms. Daniels, but after she told us we'd be spending the next two months working on self-portraits, I wasn't so sure. As far as I'm concerned, the whole point of making a painting is you can stop thinking about yourself for as long as you're working. What's the fun of an art class spent looking in the mirror?

At lunch, just as I was explaining to Madison and Jessica the difference between a still life and a portrait, Kathryn Ford came over to the table where we were sitting. She was with a girl so beautiful she actually gave Kathryn a run for her money. With her thick, curly brown hair and enormous blue eyes, she looked like a Victoria's Secret model in the flesh. This was one woman who *definitely* did not need a padded bra.

"Hey," said Kathryn. She tossed her Prada bag on the table and dropped into a chair.

"Hey," said the other girl, tossing her own Prada bag down and collapsing into a chair next to Kathryn.

"Hey," I said. Madison and Jessica said, "Hi."

"So, what's up?" Kathryn asked, like her sitting with and talking to us was something that happened every day.

"Not a whole lot," said Madison, playing the same game of pretend. "What's up with you?"

"Not much," said Kathryn. She looked over at me. "I like your shirt," she said.

"Oh, thanks." I was wearing an ancient Ramones T-shirt my dad got at a concert back before I was born. My mom had tie-dyed it all these wild, psychedelic colors. It's pretty faded now, but I still like it.

"So, you're going out with Connor," she said.

Was she asking me or telling me?

"Yeah, she's going out with Connor," Jessica piped up. She spoke defensively, like Kathryn had better watch herself.

Kathryn laughed. "Chill," she said to Jessica. Then she turned to me. "Connor's adorbs. He's practically like my brother." She laughed. "And anyway, I don't go out with high-school guys."

She laughed again, and so did the rest of us, as if the idea that Kathryn Ford would date a high-school guy was nothing short of hilarious. When we all stopped laughing,

Kathryn bumped her beautiful friend's shoulder. "No offense," she said. "None taken," purred the beautiful girl, and the two of them started laughing again.

"Anyway," Kathryn continued, "I just wanted to know if you need a ride to the game Friday."

"Oh, no," said Madison. "We're good."

Kathryn kept looking at me, as if Madison hadn't even spoken. "Thanks," I said evenly. "We're all set."

"Suit yourself," said Kathryn. She stretched her arms over her head, and her tiny tee slid up to reveal her perfectly flat stomach. "I guess we'll see you there."

"Yeah, sure," I said.

As soon as they were gone, Madison turned to me. "She is *such* a phony." She made her voice high and squeaky. "'Do you need a ride? Connor's practically my brother. I like your shirt.' God."

"I know," Jessica said. "Adorbs? *Puh-leeze.*"

I didn't say much as the conversation wound past all the ways Kathryn Ford was a phony, two-faced hypocrite who wasn't nearly as pretty as she thought she was. Because there was only one aspect of Kathryn Ford's phony, two-faced, hypocrisy that had the slightest effect on me.

I don't go out with high-school guys.

Somehow I got the feeling that if Kathryn ever decided to change her policy, I was going to be in serious trouble.

* * *

89

Friday afternoon a few people had stayed in the studio after class ended, including Sam Wolff. Except for me and Sam, everyone was talking more than they were working. Sam was focusing really hard on his painting, and I was focusing really hard on the clock, wishing the hour I'd sworn to spend drawing would pass faster. And it wasn't just because I had zero ideas for my self-portrait. All I could think about were my plans for the night. I'd take the late bus, which left at five and would get me home at five-thirty, plenty of time to shower, get dressed, and let my hair dry before Madison and Jessica picked me up at seven. Not only was tonight a crucial game for making the states, there was a huge party afterward at some senior's house. *And* the coach had promised the guys that if they won, they could have a night with no curfew. Needless to say, I wasn't going to be mentioning *that* to Mara. Just thinking of all the hours I'd get to make out with Connor gave me goose bumps. I wanted it to be five o'clock *now*.

At four fifty-five, I grabbed my bag and Connor's jacket, shoved my sketch pad in my drawer, and started for the door. As I passed his easel, I couldn't help noticing the painting Sam was working on.

"Wow," I said. It was a still life of a dining room table after a massive meal has just been consumed—there were half-eaten plates of pasta, empty serving dishes, crumpled napkins, and abandoned knives and forks. The painting was spectacular: a still life in tiny, colorful squares. I leaned in to see the squares up close and realized the designs in them weren't just designs; each was actually a tiny image. The wine bottle was made of bunches of grapes, the melting ice cubes were actually a minute, snow-capped mountain range. Stepping back from the finished section of the painting you saw the contour of each thing made from the shapes and shades within the squares. Only when you were standing right at the canvas could you see the specifics of the little images.

"That's amazing." I wanted to touch the rich, thick paint. "You know who it reminds me of? Chuck Close." Chuck Close is an artist I'd first seen years ago, when my dad and I made a pre-Mara trip to New York and went to the Museum of Modern Art. Ever since then he's been one of my favorite artists. Close does the same thing Sam had done, squares of shapes and colors that create a figurative image.

Sam didn't say anything. In fact, he didn't even look at me.

Once again I felt what I'd felt that day in the museum: the urge to put him in his place. "You know," I said, "it's customary to acknowledge when someone directly addresses you. It's called being polite."

He didn't move his eyes from his easel. "I wasn't exactly ready to have a public viewing."

The truth was Ms. Daniels always made kind of a big deal about not looking at other people's artwork before they were ready to show it.

"Oh," I said. "Well, sorry."

Sam nodded and looked back at his painting. Whatever. He probably hadn't even heard of Chuck Close. And why did he have to act like I'd gone snooping through his drawer? Would it have killed him to just say thank you? I mean, is that so much to ask for? *Thank you.*

I walked out of the room without saying good-bye, making it to the late bus just as the driver was shutting the doors.

I could hear Avril Lavigne blasting from the Princesses' room as soon as I opened the front door. Sometimes I think my stepsisters aren't actually people so much as the epicenter of some cultural Venn diagram.

As if in response to my thinking about them, both Princesses stuck their heads out of their room and, spying me in the entrance foyer, came racing down the stairs. They were wearing vaguely nautical velvet dresses.

"You guys going sailing?" I asked, hanging Connor's jacket in the closet.

Their dresses—one blue, the other red—were a kind of horrible variation on a theme. The tight velvet clung to their bodies, which lacked a crucial curve or two. Both girls wore heavy blue eye shadow and sparkles on their cheekbones, and coming down the stairs, each teetered slightly in her platform shoes. When they were just a few feet away, I saw their dresses still had the tags on them.

Princess Two was brushing Princess One's hair, which was growing increasingly frizzy with each stroke.

"Mom's *really* pissed," Princess One informed me. Then she raised her eyebrows and sighed, cultivating a bored supermodel mid-photo-shoot look.

"What are you *talking* about?" I asked, putting my hands on my hips in what I realized too late was the stance they usually took with me.

"Did you get that shirt at Marmara?" asked Princess One, distracted from the pleasure of bearing bad news by the pleasure of talking fashion.

"What?" I asked.

She rolled her eyes. "Marmara? It's only, like, the coolest store at the Miracle Mile." The Miracle Mile is a posh outdoor shopping mall a few minutes from our house. To the Princesses, it is a holy site akin to the Temple Mount in Jerusalem.

"Yeah," said Princess Two, "their stuff is *soo* nice. There's this girl in our class and—"

"OUCH!" Princess One jerked her head away and whipped around to glare at Princess Two. "You're *hurting* me."

"Well, *sorry*," Princess Two snarled. "But it's all knotted."

Princess One grabbed the brush from Princess Two. "It's not knotted. You're just a spaz. And it's going to be straightened next Saturday anyway," she said. "We just got these," she informed me, gesturing at their dresses. "For Jason Goldberg's bar mitzvah."

"We're going on the *QM Two* next week," said Princess Two.

"The *QM Two*?" I asked. "I thought you just said you were going to a bar mitzvah."

"*Hello!* The *Queen Mary Two.* It's, like, a huge ocean liner.

"I know what it is. But I thought you were going—"

"It sails to Europe," Princess One explained.

"You're sailing to Europe?"

"Duh. You can't sail to Europe and back in one night," said Princess Two. This from a girl who, just two weeks ago, lost points on a geography quiz for not knowing England is an island.

"Yeah, duh," Princess One echoed. "We're just going on the boat. For Jason Goldberg's bar mitzvah."

"It's on the *QM Two*?"

But they were tired of wowing me with their triumph on the bar mitzvah circuit.

"Mom said you didn't clean up your room and it's a federal disaster site," said Princess Two. Despite being uttered by her daughter, the words were obviously Mara's.

"Gee, maybe that's because I lack something called *furniture*," I suggested.

They shrugged and turned away in unison, two slightly unsteady runway models. "Whatev," said Princess One.

"Yeah, whatev," said Princess Two.

I grabbed an Oreo from the kitchen and went downstairs to my room. Looking around I had to admit it would not be winning the *Good Housekeeping* seal of approval anytime soon. But what was I supposed to do about that? I had no *drawers*. I had no *closet*. Surely even vile Mara could see I was doing my best to keep some semblance of order in the chaos that was my unfurnished life.

I lay on my air mattress wondering when my dad would be home and if the first thing I was going to hear from him was a clean-up-your-room lecture. If I hadn't been leaving for the game in less than an hour, I might have put together a counterargument, but given that getting grounded would put a huge crimp in my plans, I decided I'd better just suck up his lecture and agree to spend the next day doing something about the mess.

I thought about the post-game party, wondering if Connor and I would drive together or if he'd come later, like he had to Piazzolla's. I imagined him getting to the party after I was already there, how he'd find me in the crowd, come up and put his arms around me. *Hey, Red,* he'd say. *Hey, Connor,* I'd say. And then while everybody stood there, pretending not to watch, he'd give me one of his amazing kisses and I'd—

There was a knock at my door. "Lucy?" It was Mara.

This was an unexpected development. "Yeah?" I sat

up quickly, hiding the Oreo I'd been nibbling under a pillow. Mara doesn't like it when we have snacks outside of the kitchen.

She opened the door and called down. "May I speak to you for a moment?"

"Yeah, sure. Of course."

A minute later she appeared at the foot of the stairs, totally glam in stilettos and a tight black dress with a slit up one side.

"I came down here earlier today, and I was extremely surprised to see what a mess this room is." Her lips were pursed tightly together, and she had her hands folded in front of her, like everything in the room was so filthy she was afraid to touch it.

"Yeah, I know what you mean. I keep thinking I'll straighten everything up once I have, you know, drawers and stuff to put my clothes in."

She nodded her head while I spoke but kept her eyebrows raised, as if commenting on the ludicrousness of my alibi.

"Quite honestly, Lucy, I don't see how not having a few pieces of furniture is an excuse for what a mess this room has become," she said after I'd finished.

"Well, I mean I'm not *excusing* it," I said. "But it would definitely be easier to put my clothes away if I had something to put them away *in*." I slid my hand out from under the pillow, leaving the Oreo behind. Like a bird of prey, Mara followed the movement with her eyes.

She sucked on her lower lip for a second before answering. "So it's my fault that your room is a mess," she said finally.

"No, I'm not saying it's your *fault*," I said, though I didn't exactly see whose fault it was if not hers. I mean, had the woman never heard of Ikea? "I'm just saying that normally, you know, when I have a closet and a dresser and stuff, I'm a lot neater than this."

"Well, the fact is right now you *don't* have those things, and this is an unacceptable way to keep your room. I'd like to know what you're going to do about it. Or were you just planning to wait until I can make time in my busy schedule to run around and shop for furniture for you?"

I love the idea that Mara has a busy schedule. It's like getting to her weekly mani/pedi and hair coloring appointment makes her the CEO of a multinational corporation.

"But, Mara, you didn't want me to bring my stuff from San Francisco, and you keep saying you want to be the one to furnish the house, so I don't see how I can go out and buy myself furniture." Not to mention my lack of a car and several hundred dollars of disposable income.

"I'm not sure I like your using that tone of voice, Lucy," said Mara, taking a step toward the bed and pointing at me. In spite of myself, I leaned away from her advance.

"I'm not taking a tone," I said. "I'm just stating a fact."

"Hello?" It was my dad calling from upstairs. "I'm home! Where is everybody?"

"I'm down here, Doug," Mara called. I'd been about to say, *I'm in my room, Dad*, but instead I just sat there.

He came bounding down the stairs, giving a low whistle when he saw Mara's dress. "Hi, honey," he said. Wearing jeans and a worn gray sweater, he looked relaxed and happy, like he was really glad to be home. He kissed Mara hello and then came over and kissed me.

"How was your week?" he asked. Mara's joining in our phone conversations had finally gotten too annoying to bear, so after Monday I'd just avoided talking to him when he'd called.

"We seem to have a little bit of a problem," said Mara, before I could answer him.

"Oh, yeah, what's that?" he asked, dancing toward her and slipping his arm around her waist. "They found a cure for diabetes and the benefit's off?" Ever since we moved to New York, Mara's been dragging my dad to all these fund-raisers. In theory, she hopes to cure every scourge that threatens the planet. In fact, she just wants to show off her new man on the charity circuit.

"Lucy seems to be under the impression it's my fault her room is such a mess," Mara said.

"That is so not true!" I said. "I just said I couldn't

put my clothes away until I had some furniture to put them away *in*."

"And then she took a very snotty tone that I did not appreciate," Mara continued, ignoring me.

"Oh my god, it's like unless I'm kowtowing to you every second I'm taking a snotty tone," I said. I could feel tears brewing and I choked them back.

"Hey, hey!" said my dad, who wasn't smiling anymore. "I just got home. I don't want all this fighting." He put his arm around Mara. "Lucy, I'd like you to apologize to Mara, and I want this room straightened up."

"I'm going to straighten it up. I'll straighten it up tomorrow."

"No," said my dad, "you'll straighten it up tonight."

"Dad, I'm supposed to go to a basketball game tonight."

I was sure I could see my dad hesitating, but then he said, "I'm sorry, but you're not going out tonight."

"*WHAT?!*" It almost wasn't a word, just a strangled yelp.

"We want this room cleaned up, and we want it cleaned up tonight." The way my dad said "we" as they stood next to each other, his arm around Mara's waist, only highlighted how the two of them comprised a perfectly coordinated team. I suddenly felt very conscious of being the only person on my side of the room.

"Why can't I just clean it up tomorrow? If you let

me go to the game, I promise I'll get up early and clean everything." I was fighting back panic.

My dad was about to relent, I could tell. He'd never been one of those parents who cared what my room looked like, and I knew he wouldn't mind if I cleaned up in the morning. But just as he opened his mouth to say something, Mara spoke.

"Lucy, your father and I said tonight, and we mean tonight," she said, turning on one heel and heading upstairs. My dad took a step toward me just as Mara said, "Doug, we're going to be late."

He hesitated a second and then said, "I'll see you in the morning, Goose."

"What?" I said, and I was crying for real now. "Are you saying this conversation is over?"

"There's no conversation," he said. "We asked you to do something and we want you do to it."

The way he repeated *we* almost took my breath away.

"And that's all you have to say?" I asked finally.

"Lucy, I'm sorry," he said. "But you need to do what you're told." Then he, too, turned around and headed up the stairs.

Trying to stop crying, I picked up my cell and dialed Connor's number.

"Yo, what's up? It's Connor. You know what to do."

"Um, hey, Connor, I—" a sob almost escaped, and I took a deep breath. "I can't come to the game tonight.

I—this whole thing happened at home, and I'm grounded. I'm really sorry. So, good luck and . . . have fun at the party." The last part of my message nearly pushed me over the edge. I hit END CALL as quickly as I could. Then I dialed Jessica's number.

"*It's Jessica. Leave me a message and I'll call you back.*"

"Hi. It's me. My stepmother is trying to win some kind of bitch-of-the-year award, and I'm grounded tonight. So have fun for both of us."

After I hung up I sat staring at my cell for a long minute, wondering what happens if Cinderella never makes it to the ball. Does Prince Charming spend the night pining away for her, crying into his royal beer? Or does he just meet someone else, some girl who doesn't have a wicked, stepdaughter-grounding stepmother?

Some girl who no longer doesn't "go out with high school guys"?

The answer was too obvious. I turned my phone off and shoved it into my bag. That way I wouldn't have to listen to it *not* ringing all night long.

Chapter Eleven

I'd forced myself not to check my messages before I went to bed, knowing how bad I'd feel if Connor hadn't called. But the first thing I did when I woke up in my immaculate room was check voice mail.

Two messages. My hands shook so much I could hardly manage to dial in for them.

"Hey, Red." I let out a tiny, involuntary scream. "Do you need me to take out a hit on one of your family members? 'Cause I'll do it." Just the sound of his voice made last night's fight with my dad seem like a bad dream. "You better not be grounded all weekend, Red. I'm picking you up at seven on Saturday and taking you out for dinner."

I played the message three more times before saving it. The second call was from Jessica. "Can I just say that your stepmother totally gets my vote for bitch-of-the-year? Call me when you wake up. We're going shopping tomorrow." I played that message again, too.

Guess what, Mara, not everyone takes your side, you dumb cow.

I'd barely hung up the phone when it rang. "Hello?"

"We'll be at your house in twenty minutes," said Jessica. "We're going to Miracle Mile."

"Connor's taking me out to dinner tonight," I said.

Jessica screamed. "Oh my god! He *loves* you."

I couldn't think of what to say to that, so I just screamed. Then I remembered something. "Jessica, I don't have anything to wear."

"Okay, do not panic," said Jessica. "They don't call it Miracle Mile for nothing."

Madison's mom dropped us off at Bistro des Filles for lunch, where Madison, after telling us how many millions of grams of fat were in each of the entrées we'd ordered, just got a glass of water. Then she ate about two-thirds of Jessica's Croque Monsieur before Jessica threatened to stab her with a fork if she didn't get her own sandwich.

By four o'clock, despite my duet of personal shoppers, I still didn't have anything to wear on my date with Connor. Madison and Jessica dismissed everything I liked as boring, while everything they wanted me to try on cost about a thousand times what I'd planned on spending. Finally, since we were running out of time, we agreed to split up. Madison went to Chanel to get a mascara, while Jessica and I headed to Ralph Lauren to look for a dress for me.

As soon as we walked in the door, I saw Jessica notice a blue linen tank top and hesitate for a second before continuing past the rack.

"That's nice," I said. "You should try it on."

She shook her head. "We're here to find you a date-worthy dress."

But I nudged her toward the top. "Go for it," I said.

"Are you sure you don't mind waiting?" she asked. "I'll be *really* fast."

"I'm sure," I said. "Take your time." While Jessica went to look for a dressing room, I wandered around looking for something I could possibly wear on my date. But unless Connor was taking me for a cruise on his yacht, there was nothing in Ralph Lauren that would be right. Finally I gave up; in a wood-paneled alcove stocked with evening dresses, I found an empty chair and collapsed into it, dropping my head back, closing my eyes, and sighing.

"I don't know," said a familiar voice, "you're the one who told *me* what black-tie means."

My eyes snapped open. Sitting a few feet away from me was the last person in the world I'd have expected to find in the evening-dress section of the Ralph Lauren store at the Miracle Mile.

Sam Wolff.

He was hunched forward over a sketch pad, and he didn't see me. In his faded jeans and a torn Red Grooms T-shirt, he looked a little out of place sitting on the overstuffed chintz chair. But he didn't seem self-conscious, like most of the other guys who were sitting around waiting for their wives or girlfriends to show off a dress they were considering buying. Instead he looked totally oblivious to his surroundings, like he could just as easily have been on the Left Bank of the Seine or the median of the Long Island Expressway. While I was watching, he pulled absently on a corkscrew curl at the back of his head, then suddenly let it go and drew a series of lines on the page.

Just as I turned to look around for Jessica, the door to the dressing room right in front of where Sam was sitting flew open to reveal the beautiful girl who'd sat down at my table that day with Kathryn Ford. The slinky black cocktail dress she was wearing showed off her amazing body.

"Okay, this or the green one?" she asked. To my amazement, she was addressing Sam.

He didn't look up. "Eeny, meeny, miny, moe," he said, still sketching.

"Sam," she said, "you're starting to piss me off."

He sighed and flipped his sketch pad closed.

"Okay," he said. "Turn around." She spun around on her heel. "The green one." Considering how gorgeous she looked in the dress she was wearing, I couldn't even begin to fathom what the green one must have looked like.

"Oh, please," she said. "You have the worst taste."

"And you're asking my opinion because . . ."

"Just forget it, okay?" She looked at herself in the mirror, frowning, though what she could possibly have seen that made her frown was completely beyond me. "Obviously, if I want this done right, I'm going to have to do it myself."

"Jane, you're gorgeous in everything you tried on, up to and including the very first dress I saw you in *three hours ago*."

Now I was starting to feel weird about how thoroughly I was eavesdropping. What if Sam suddenly turned around and saw me?

"Could you just be quiet for a minute? I can't even hear myself think." She studied herself in the mirror. "I hate this stupid rehearsal dinner, I hate this stupid wedding, and I hate my stupid sister."

"Amen to that," said Sam, flipping his sketch pad open again.

She shot him a look. "I'm getting both and I'll decide at home," she said. Then she opened the dressing-room door and disappeared behind it just as Jessica appeared holding a shopping bag. "There you are," she said. "Oh, hey, Sam."

Sam turned around lazily. I froze, sure he'd be all, *Enjoying listening in on my conversation much?* But the only thing he said was, "Hey." Then he kind of lifted his head in my direction in a move that was somewhere between a nod and a nothing.

Now I was totally confused. How did Sam not only know A) the most beautiful girl in the senior class, but also B) Jessica?

Jessica put her hand on my shoulder. "So we should probably hook up with Madison," she said.

"Yeah, let's go," I said. I stood up, and the ache in my feet that had disappeared while I was sitting came back.

"See you," Jessica said to Sam. Without really looking up from his pad, he gave us a salute. When we got outside, I was about to ask how she knew Sam, but she beat me to it.

"He's in my art class," I said. "But you know what's really weird? I think he was there with that girl who hangs out with Kathryn Ford."

"Oh yeah," she said. "Jane Brown. They go out."

I almost tripped over a nonexistent crack on the sidewalk. Sam Wolff, the most antisocial person on the planet, had a supermodel girlfriend?

"She's such a mega-bitch," said Jessica. "But guys totally love her. Can you believe that of all the hot guys at Glen Lake she picked some random junior artist who's a total freak?"

Something about the way Jessica said *artist* and *freak* rubbed me the wrong way. I thought of Sam's beautiful paintings and stopped walking. "What's freaky about being an artist?"

Jessica shifted her bag to her other hand. "Oh, no offense," she said, putting her hand on my arm. "I didn't mean he was a freak *because* he's an artist. I just meant . . . He, like, never talks or anything. Why would she want to go out with him?"

We started walking again. "I don't know," I said, remembering the scene in the store. "If she's such a bitch, maybe it's weird that *he* goes out with *her*."

"Is he, like, a friend of yours?" asked Jessica. "Because you're being kind of defensive about him."

"No, we're not friends." Suddenly I realized Jessica was right; I *was* being defensive about Sam. Which was pretty weird considering our total lack of anything that would resemble a friendship. "He, like, *never* talks to me," I admitted.

"Well, don't feel bad," said Jessica. She spotted Madison walking toward us and waved. "Like I said, he's a total freak."

"I *don't* feel bad," I said. "I don't even care." It was true. I didn't care. I was about to tell Jessica about how rude Sam had been to me that day at the museum when she grabbed my shoulder.

"Oh my god, look!" she said. She was pointing at a red minidress in the window of Zinna, the store right next to Ralph Lauren.

Before I could respond, Madison came up to where

we were standing. "Hey," she said. Then she saw the dress. "Wow, that's hot," she said.

"You would look *so* good in that dress," Jessica said to me.

I pointed at my hair. "Red," I said. Then I pointed at the dress. "No," I said.

"Come *on*," said Jessica. "Redheads can *totally* wear red. Try it on."

"Connor would *die* if you wore that to dinner," said Madison.

"Yeah, so would my dad," I said. Were they serious? The dress was smaller than my cell phone.

"Just try it on," said Jessica.

"Yeah," said Madison. "What do you have to lose?"

I let them pull me into the store and waited while the saleslady found the dress in my size. They stood on either side of me talking about how sexy the dress was and how great I was going to look in it, while I pretended to be considering purchasing it.

Once I'd put the dress on, I didn't even need a mirror to confirm what I already knew: there was no way I was going to buy it. Looking down, I saw that the neckline plunged below my bra, and I could feel how the tiny skirt barely grazed my thighs. Not to mention the color. I stepped out of the dressing room.

Jessica and Madison both gasped. "Oh my god," said Madison, jumping up and down. "That is *soooo* sexy."

I turned away from her to see myself in the full-length mirror. For a second I was sure I was looking at someone else's reflection.

"Lovely," said the saleswoman. "So mature. And it's on sale. Fifty percent off."

"Guys," I said, waving my hand in front of their faces. "I can't buy this dress."

"You *have* to get it," said Jessica. "You look amazing in it."

"Yeah," said Madison. "If I looked that thin in a dress, I'd totally buy it."

"It's a beautiful dress," said the saleslady.

I looked back at myself in the mirror. It was like I'd been transformed into my incredibly sexy older sister. Or maybe my incredibly slutty older sister. I turned around. You could see the lines of my underwear through the tight fabric.

"Come here," said the saleslady, beckoning me over with her finger. When I got to where she was standing, she spun me around and in one move, unclasped my bra, slipped the straps off my shoulder, and whipped it off. "There," she said. "Much better." Then she pointed at my butt. "Also, you need a thong."

"A *thong*?"

"Yes," she said. "A thong is—"

"I know what it *is*," I said quickly. "I just don't own one."

"Oh, we'll go to Lace Escapes," Madison said. Then she started to giggle.

Jessica giggled, too. "Yeah," she said, giggling harder, "they have really nice stuff."

Their laughter was contagious. "Guys, stop," I said, laughing. "I don't know . . ."

But I did know.

I was getting it.

Jessica's mom pulled up in her car just as the three of us were stepping out of Lace Escapes. She honked and waved. "Hi, girls," she called. Then she pointed at Jessica's bag. "What'd you get?"

Jessica waved at her mom. "I got the cutest tank top at Ralph Lauren. You're gonna love it."

"Oh good, honey. I can't wait to see it," said Mrs. Johnson. Then she smiled at me and I smiled back. A lot of teenagers get stressed out about meeting peoples' parents, but it doesn't bother me. I do parents really well—they always tell my dad what a nice girl I am, how I'm so polite and everything. For a second, though, while Mrs. Johnson was smiling in my direction, I felt a nervous flutter. I was afraid she was going to ask me what *I'd* gotten, and I'd have to say, "Oh, you know, just a sexy red dress and a lace thong."

It wasn't quite the nice-girl impression I was eager to make.

Chapter Twelve

Just before seven, Princess One let out a shriek that penetrated the floorboards of the living room—where she and her sister were sitting by the window waiting for Connor—and reverberated through the basement—where I was standing in front of the mirror waiting for Connor.

"He drives a Lexus!"

"That is so cool," Princess Two screamed down to me. "A Lexus is a very cool car."

I didn't care what car Connor was driving; I was just relieved he hadn't stood me up. But I couldn't take much time to thank my fairy godmother right at that particular moment, as I was in the midst of negotiating what could only be described as an extremely tricky thong situation.

The lady at Lace Escapes had assured me the thong I'd

gotten was the most comfortable one on the market. "You won't even feel it," she'd said about ten thousand times.

But how can you not feel something that keeps going up your butt? And not only does it keep going up your butt, it's *supposed* to keep going up your butt.

I shimmied, hoping to get the thong to relocate, but it didn't help. Maybe I just needed to take it off. But then what if we got in a car accident and the paramedics discovered that under my tiny little red dress I wasn't wearing any underwear? Maybe they'd decide any girl who was that big of a slut didn't deserve to live.

The bell rang and I heard the Princesses shout, "We'll get it! We'll get it!" I didn't move.

The longer I stood there, the more convinced I became that I needed to start from scratch—just take off the thong *and* the dress and wear something normal like . . .

But of course that was the problem. Normal like *what*? Normal like jeans and a T-shirt? Because if the dress came off, that was pretty much all there was to choose from. I did my little "Thong, Please Get Out of My Butt" dance again. Something somewhere must have shifted because for a second I was able to concentrate on something other than my posterior. Unfortunately, that something was my toes, which were pinched together in a pair of shoes I'd bought for (and hadn't worn since) my dad and Mara's engagement party—a night on which I'd been in so much emotional pain my aching feet had barely registered.

I looked at my reflection. The older girl in the mirror who shrugged back at me didn't look nearly as uncomfortable as I felt. Actually, she looked kind of cool and sexy. I stood up straighter. As long as I didn't have to walk more than ten yards, I'd probably be okay. I smiled, checking to see if there was any lipstick on my teeth. Then I bent over, ran my hands through my hair, and fluffed the ends like I'd seen Jessica do. It looked good.

Unfortunately, it didn't feel good. Bending over had caused the thong to shift westward again.

Walking through the dining room, I could hear Connor talking, and when I got a view of the foyer, I saw that the Princesses were standing one on either side of him, staring silently up at his beautiful face. I guess they were too young to appreciate how great his body looked in a pair of khakis and a dark blue sweater.

Connor saw me and whistled. "Hey, gorgeous," he said, looking me up and down. "Now, that's a dress." The Princesses looked over at me, and then Princess One nodded at Princess Two.

"You look pretty, Lucy," said Princess One.

I wasn't sure if they were going to follow up the compliment with an insult ("Yeah, pretty *slutty*"). When neither of them added anything, I said, "Thanks." They returned to gazing adoringly at Connor.

Just then my dad and Mara came downstairs. She was wearing an apron, as if she'd been slaving away at the stove all day, when really she'd spent the better part of the afternoon getting dressed, before throwing some tinfoil-covered catered platters into the oven. As she came toward us, she removed her apron, exposing her tiny, pink silk dress, which didn't look all that different from mine. This could not be a good sign, but I couldn't figure out which of us shouldn't have been dressed the way she was.

My dad did a double take when he saw what I was wearing, and for a second I was sure he was going to tell me there was no way I was leaving the house looking like that. I almost wished he would—my toes were throbbing. But then he just stuck out his hand. "You must be Connor," he said. "It's nice to meet you."

"Nice to meet you, sir," said Connor, and even though it was a cheesy thing to say, I was glad Connor had said it. I wanted tonight to be perfect, even if perfect meant full of clichés, like Connor calling my dad sir.

"Lucy's told us so much about you," said Mara. This was a total lie. I hadn't even mentioned Connor to Mara, and I'd barely told my dad anything about him, just said I was going out on a date with a guy on the basketball team whose name was Connor. "Won't you come join us for a drink?" she asked. She tucked his hand under her arm and led him through the arch that separates the entrance foyer from the living room.

"Actually, we should probably get going," I said to their retreating backs.

"Don't worry, we'll make it a quick drink," she said, laughing. She still had her hand on his, practically stapling it to her arm. My dad followed them, and after a second, I did, too.

"What would you like, dear?" she asked, leading Connor over to the sofa. She was being so solicitous I thought she might actually help him sit down, but at the last second she let him take care of that on his own. "Shall I mix you a martini?" She laughed again, like she'd just heard the most amusing joke in the world.

Connor told her he'd have a Coke.

"Doug, honey, will you be a darling and get Connor a Coke?" While Mara might be willing to take people's drink orders, she sure isn't going to hustle into the kitchen to fill them.

"Sure thing," said my dad, smiling.

I headed for one of the wing chairs, but as I attempted to sit, I suddenly realized my dress was really short. Like, *extremely* short. Like, you'd-better-not-sit-down-unless-you're-prepared-to-share-your-thong-with-the-entire-room short. I ended up sort of sliding onto the edge of the chair and crossing my legs tightly, balancing my weight on my left foot.

Mara turned in my direction. "Lucy, what would you like?"

"I'm fine," I said. She seated herself next to Connor on the sofa, and a second later both Princesses came in and sat down, something I'd never seen them do in all the months I'd lived with them. Had the World Wide Web crashed, leaving them without access to instant messaging for the evening?

"So, you play basketball?" Mara asked, which answered my question of whether or not my dad had told her Connor was on the team. "You know, Lucy's a huge basketball fan." She smiled across the room at me. "Aren't you, Lucy?"

Was I really supposed to answer her question? Since she continued to smile at me and didn't say anything else, I figured I was. "Sure am," I said, giving her a tight smile. She turned back to Connor.

"It's unusual to see a girl so obsessed with sports," she said.

Unusual? Obsessed? I felt my hands clenching into fists.

"Yeah, it's really cool," said Connor. I couldn't tell if he'd deliberately misunderstood her insult or was sticking up for me on purpose, but either way, Mara suddenly decided to take a different approach.

"Living with her and her father, I'm actually starting to care about the sport myself," she said. "I must be getting infected with March Madness."

The only March Madness I'd seen Mara infected with was her insane desire to lose five pounds off her already skeletal frame before bathing-suit season.

"Yeah," said Princess Two, "Lucy makes it seem like basketball is really interesting. I want her to teach me all

117

about it." She actually had the audacity to look at me as she said this, neglecting to mention that in December she'd suggested I might be A) so tall and B) so interested in basketball because of an undiagnosed hormonal imbalance.

"Drinks are served," said my dad, coming in with a tray. Princess One leaped to her feet; skipping around the coffee table to grab the Coke for Connor, she just missed impaling herself on a glass figurine.

"Thanks," he said, smiling at her.

"Okay," she said, not quite looking at him. Then she went back to the tray, which didn't have any glasses on it now that my dad and Mara had both taken their drinks.

"Lucy, don't you want a drink?" she asked. "I'll get you one."

Connor was smiling at Princess One with that look people get when they're simultaneously amused and touched by a child's excellent manners. I, on the other hand, was smiling at her with that look people get when they're pretty sure someone they know well has been replicated by aliens.

"I'm fine," I said, my teeth clenched. Then in spite of myself I added, "Thank you."

"You're welcome," she said. "If you change your mind, just let me know."

This was all getting to be a little too much for me, and I stood up. "We should go," I said.

"But Connor hasn't even had a chance to drink his Coke," said Mara, touching him on the sleeve.

My flesh crawled.

"That's okay, Mrs. Norton," said Connor, taking a big swig and smiling at her. "Lucy's right." He stood up, and the Princesses jumped to their feet. After a second, my dad and Mara both stood up, too.

"It was nice meeting you," Connor said to my father.

"You too," said my dad. He looked from me to Mara like he wished we weren't dressed quite so identically. Then he shook Connor's hand again. "Enjoy your dinner," he said to him.

"Yes," said Mara, taking his hand and half holding, half shaking it. "Enjoy your dinner." Then she looked over at me and back at Connor. "And take care of our girl."

Now I was glad I hadn't had anything to drink; my empty stomach was the only thing that kept me from puking all over her.

"I will, Mrs. Norton," he said. "And thanks for the Coke." He looked over to the Princesses. "It was great to meet you girls."

"You too," said Princess One. Princess Two just sighed.

Everyone walked us to the door and waited while I reached into the closet and grabbed Connor's jacket. "Well, bye," I said.

Even with an antique breakfront the size of the

Titanic against one wall, the entryway is pretty big, but with everyone huddled around us I practically had to step outside to have enough room to put the jacket on.

"Bye, Lucy," said the Princesses.

"Good-bye, kids," said my dad. "Have fun."

Mara just waved and smiled at us, like a contestant in a beauty contest. When we were in the car with the doors closed, Connor turned to me before putting the key in the ignition.

"Wow," he said, "you have an awesome family."

I was about to tell him my "family" is about as awesome as the Mansons, but as I opened my mouth to explain what a farce he'd just witnessed, he leaned toward me. "Good to see you, Red," he said.

And right then, facing the mighty power of Connor's delicious kisses, the lecture I'd been about to deliver on the duplicitous nature of pure evil was lost forever.

As Connor and I drove to the restaurant, I started to feel nervous. Technically, this was our first date. True, we'd gone out before. But we hadn't been alone. What if we didn't have anything to talk about over dinner? What if we just sat there, staring at each other across the table in total silence? But then Connor started talking, explaining that he was driving his dad's car because a warning light had suddenly lit up on the dashboard of his SUV. When he finished the story, he popped in a CD, cranked the volume, and dropped a hand onto my knee. A minute later, he took my hand and ran his thumb across the back of it.

My terror that we'd pass the night in silence ebbed, replaced by the most powerful sensation of disbelief I'd ever experienced. Was this really happening to me? More than anything, I wished I could show a preview of this moment to my desperate, lonely, first-semester self.

Connor found a space right in front of the restaurant, a Japanese place called Osaka, and before we got out of the car, we started kissing. I would have been perfectly happy if we hadn't made it to dinner, but after a couple of minutes, Connor pulled away.

"I'm starving, Red." He pulled the keys out of the ignition and popped open his door. "Lez eat!"

Suffering from my usual post-kissing-Connor confusion, I took a little longer to extricate myself from the car than he did. By the time I'd unbuckled my seat belt and maneuvered onto the sidewalk, Connor was standing by the door of the restaurant, holding it open for me.

Inside Osaka there were regular tables and, toward the back, low tables at which people sat on pillows with their legs crossed Indian style.

"Good evening," said the hostess, walking toward us carrying two menus. "Would you prefer to sit Western or Japanese style?" When she said "Japanese style" she gestured toward one of the low tables.

"Western," I practically shouted. She nodded, and Connor and I followed her to a regular table against the wall. I sat down normally, grateful to have a tablecloth between the world and my thong.

"God, I love sushi," I said. "I don't think I've had it since we left San Francisco. My dad and I used to eat it practically every other night."

"Oh, yeah? That's cool, Red," he said. I looked down the menu. Yellowtail. Shrimp. Tuna. I hadn't even realized how much I missed my regular sushi infusions until this minute.

"Ready?" asked the waitress. She flipped open her pad and held her pen ready.

"Take it away, Red," said Connor.

"Um, I'll have two pieces of yellowtail, an unagi, a shrimp, and the special hand roll," I said. She nodded, getting it all down. Then she turned to Connor.

"Wow, Red," he said. "You're daring. I'll have the steak teriyaki." He snapped his menu shut and handed it to her.

"Have you ever tried sushi?" I asked him as soon as the waitress had gone.

"Raw fish? No way," he said. He made a cross with his chopsticks as if to ward off vampires. I was about to ask him why not, when the thought occurred to me that perhaps I should change the subject rather than continuing to call his attention to the fact that I was about to eat food he apparently found as revolting as the undead.

"Sorry you had to go through that whole scene back at my house," I said. I wanted him to know what Mara and the Princesses were really like. "They never act that way."

Before I could explain what I meant, Connor slipped his fingers through mine. "Don't worry about it, Red. Your family's nice. And your mom's so cool. I can see where you get your great legs." He smiled and squeezed my hand.

"She's not my mother," I practically shouted. The idea that someone could think Mara was my mother made me sick to my stomach. "She's my stepmother." Even the word itself had come to have something black and spidery about it. I took my hand from Connor's and wiped my now-sweaty fingers on my napkin, which, though Mara was absent, I'd put on my lap as soon as we sat down.

"Gotcha," said Connor. I was glad he didn't start asking a million questions about my family. I mean, I guess my boyfriend needs to know that his girl-friend lives with her dad and her wicked stepmother because her mother is dead. But I wasn't exactly anxious to bring up a subject that would undoubtedly be a huge downer.

Connor took a sip of his water and so did I. As soon as I put the glass back on the table, a waiter magically appeared at my elbow and refilled it.

"Thanks," I said. He nodded and slipped away.

"Hey, did you watch the game last night?" Connor asked, chewing on some ice.

"The Knicks or the—"

"No, the Syracuse game."

"Yeah," I said. "I felt like they just folded in the fourth quarter. Everybody's been saying they have this unstoppable offense, but I thought they were totally lame."

"Totally," he agreed, taking some ice out of his glass with a fork. "Did you watch all the way to the end? Did you see how they missed that last shot?"

I nodded and made a face. "It was tragic," I agreed.

As we discussed the game and who we thought would make it to the NCAA finals, I started to get a strange feeling about the conversation. It was as if basketball was this tiny island of talk Connor and I were standing on, and if we tried to step off it, we'd drown in a sea of silence. By the time our food came, I was sure we couldn't possibly have any more basketball-related items to discuss, but then Connor got onto the subject of the Glen Lake team, and how this year they were better than they'd ever been.

Unfortunately, I couldn't really focus on what he was saying, only it wasn't because I didn't know most of the people he was talking about. The second I leaned forward to take my first bite of sushi, the strap of my dress slipped off my shoulder, almost taking the entire right side of the top with it. I dropped the piece of yellowtail I'd been about to taste and grabbed at my dress, firmly pulling it back up. Then I took a deep breath and, bending forward as little as possible, got the yellowtail back on my chopsticks. As I dropped my chin to get the piece in my mouth, the strap started slipping again, and when I grabbed for it, a clump of rice dropped off my chopsticks and slipped down the front of my dress. I felt it lodge between my breasts, right where a tiny decorative rose might have nestled if I'd been wearing a bra.

I panicked. Should I try to remove it? How do you reach down the front of your dress and subtly pull out a rice meteor? Maybe the best thing to do was just leave it there and hope it went away by itself. But what if it "went away" by heading south? I could see it now. I'd stand up, and a second later a golf ball of rice would drop onto my chair. I'd look like Long-Eared Peter, the rabbit we had in my second-grade classroom, who dropped little pellets wherever he went.

This particular image occupied a not-insignificant part of my brain for most of dinner. I kept lightly stroking my chest just above the top of the dress, hoping to find an opportune moment to plunge my hand into the bodice and remove the offending rice ball.

The problem with my plan was that Connor's eyes were glued to my hand, which I realized too late was like a pointer directing his gaze to my (basically non-existent) cleavage. If he hadn't dropped his fork halfway through the meal and needed to look around for a waiter to get him a new one, I might have had to remain seated for the rest of my life. Luckily, the three seconds during which he was distracted were all I needed to lean forward enough to loosen the tight fabric, grab the rice out of my dress, and drop it next to my pile of wasabi.

"May I take your plates?" asked our waitress.

"Yeah, sure," said Connor, dropping his napkin on the table and stretching. "That was delicious."

I nodded in agreement as the waitress expertly cleared the table.

"Some dessert?"

Connor shook his head at her and then looked across the table at me, "I'm sorry, Red. Now that we might make the states, Coach is insane about us being home by ten when there's no game. He called Matt's house last week to check up on him."

"Don't worry about it," I said. "I'm stuffed."

"I'll bring the check," said the waitress.

As we sat there, Connor stroked the back of my hand, and I felt the tingles I always got when he touched me. "That dress is really hot," he said.

His look made the whole rice fiasco suddenly worthwhile. "Thanks," I said.

"Wow, I've been yapping away," said Connor, smiling at me. "You're a really good listener."

That smile. It made me dizzy. "Thanks," I said again.

"But I want to know more about you," he said, turning my hand over and pressing his palm into mine.

"What do you want to know?" I asked, suddenly anxious. I should have prepared some funny anecdotes about myself. What could be more boring than a person just launching into her life story? *Well, I was born in Los Angeles, and after my mother died when I was three . . .* Connor would be asleep before I hit fourth grade.

Luckily, just as I was considering narrating an imaginary but fascinating childhood posted in port cities around the globe, the waitress brought our check. Connor took out his credit card and handed it over. His casual confidence as he dealt with the check was sexy; it made him seem older. Not so old that it was gross he was going out with a high-school girl, though. He seemed just older enough.

"Thank you for dinner," I said. It came out more formal than I'd meant it to, as if I were thanking my friend's dad or something.

Connor didn't seem to mind, though. He raised an eyebrow at me. "Sure, Red. But I still owe you a dessert." It sounded flirtatious, like we were talking about something way more intimate than gelato.

"Maybe *I* owe *you* a dessert," I said. I hoped I sounded flirtatious, too, and not like I'd been tallying up what each of us had spent on the other.

Connor gave me his killer smile. "All the dessert I need is you in that dress," he said. Then he let out a howl like a werewolf.

We both laughed, and when the waitress brought

the credit card slip for Connor to sign, we were still laughing. When we finally stopped laughing he said, "You're hilarious, Red," even though he was the one who'd made the joke. It made me feel witty and amusing.

At the door, Connor helped me into my (his) jacket, and outside he leaned me up against the car door and we started making out. His tongue traced a line from my ear to my collar bone. I wished we'd just skipped dinner and spent the whole night in his car fooling around, but it's not exactly like you can suggest something like that.

The whole ride home Connor held my hand; luckily he had to fix the equalizer on the stereo a couple of times, so I was able to wipe my palm on my dress before it could get too sweaty. And he didn't just hold my hand like it was a rock he'd happened to drop his hand down on. He held it perfectly, tracing my fingers with his thumb and then squeezing my hand into a fist, or brushing his fingers over my knuckles. I didn't know what Connor's career plans were, but he could definitely get rich teaching other guys how to hold a girl's hand.

When we pulled up in front of my house, Connor kissed me lightly on the lips. "Thanks for understanding about curfew, Red," he said. "Even if we make the states, it's only a few more weeks, and then we can stay out until dawn. And I expect you to wear that dress." He lifted my hand up to his lips and kissed it.

Since I planned to set fire to my dress as soon as I

got inside, Connor probably wouldn't be seeing it again. I didn't mention that, though, especially since staying out until dawn with Connor sounded like a fine idea to me. We sat in the car, kissing, until the clock on the dashboard read nine fifty-five.

"I gotta go, Red," he said softly.

"Yeah," I said. I remembered to undo my seat belt before I opened the car door.

"I'll call you tomorrow," he said. I shut the door and waved; before he pulled away, he mimed howling at the moon.

When I got into bed, I closed my eyes and replayed Connor's kisses in my mind. Then I got out of bed, grabbed my iPod, and replayed them again, this time to music. I turned out the light and snuggled under the covers, leaving the music on. I closed my eyes, feeling Connor's hands on my face, his lips gently tracing the curve of my ear. The last song I heard before I fell asleep was "Little Red Corvette." I tried to figure out why it was the perfect sound track for the night, and when I came up with the answer, I almost laughed out loud.

Of course it was perfect.

It was Prince.

Chapter Thirteen

Connor called me during the South Carolina game on Sunday, and we "watched" the whole second half together. Later he called again, and we stayed on the phone until the end of the pre-game show, when he had to get off because he'd told his dad they'd watch the game together. Monday right after first period, he came up behind me, put his hands over my eyes, and whispered in my ear, "Guess who," and I felt my stomach drop with familiar excitement. I turned to face him, wrapped my arms tightly around his waist, and we backed into a locker as some guy I didn't know called out, "Get a room." I could feel Connor smiling, but he didn't stop kissing me until the warning bell rang.

"Catch you later," I said, pulling away and raising my eyebrow at him.

"Not if I catch you first," he said.

It was weird, though—I seemed to be leading two separate lives. At school, I was never alone. When I sat down in one of my classes, within seconds, two or three people were competing for every desk in the vicinity of mine. At lunch, Madison, Jessica, and I sat squeezed together while people who'd ignored me for two-thirds of the year clamored for a seat at our table. Sometimes when we had classes in totally different parts of the building, Connor would call me on my cell between periods, so I'd be talking on the phone to him *and* to whomever I was walking with. There weren't enough hours in the school day for me to see and talk to everyone who wanted to see and talk to me.

But my fairy godmother must have forgotten to sprinkle her magic dust over my house, because whenever I happened to be home in the evening, Mara and my stepsisters were either out or they completely ignored me. Not that I cared. I just couldn't help noticing.

The Friday after my sushi dinner with Connor, my dad got home while Mara was driving the Princesses over to their dad's house. He walked in the door just as I was taking Connor's jacket out of the closet in the entrance foyer.

"Hey, Goose," he said, dropping his garment bag and giving me a hug.

"Hey," I said, hugging him back.

He looked me up and down. I was wearing jeans and a pale yellow T-shirt.

131

"Now I may not know much about fashion, but I have to say I really prefer this to that red dress of yours."

I shrugged as if I couldn't really see the difference.

He slipped his briefcase off his shoulder and grabbed a hanger out of the closet. "You want to watch the game tomorrow afternoon?" he asked, hanging up his coat. "I could pick up a pizza. Or we could pop some of that really disgusting buttery microwave popcorn."

Just then a cab pulled up in front of the house and honked. I could see Madison and Jessica sitting in the backseat. "Can't," I said. "I'm watching the game over at Connor's."

My dad slid the closet door shut. "You know, I feel a little strange that we haven't even talked about this new relationship," he said.

I folded my arms across my chest and tapped my foot. I mean, could he not see that my friends were outside waiting for me? "What do you want to talk about?"

"I don't know," he said. He scratched his head and smiled at me. "Are you okay? Mara says she practically never sees you during the week."

I snorted. That was a good one. Maybe he should have tried asking her *why* she never saw me during the week. "I'm fine, Dad," I said.

He put his hand on my shoulder. "That's great," he said, giving me a squeeze. "We just haven't talked in a while, that's all."

The cab honked again. "I really gotta go," I said.

"Yeah, sure," he said, but he didn't let go of my shoulder. I had to slip out from under his hand to get to the door.

"Well, maybe we'll watch together on Sunday."

"Yeah, maybe," I said, putting on Connor's jacket and pushing the glass door open.

But I knew I couldn't watch the game with my dad Sunday. I had a ton of work I needed to get done.

I waved to Madison and Jessica, and hurried toward the cab.

I basically didn't see my dad before he left for San Francisco Sunday night. I didn't see much of Mara or the Princesses in the days that followed either, which might explain why nobody gave me a heads-up about the bed that magically appeared in my room sometime between when I left for school Wednesday morning and when I returned home Wednesday afternoon. It wasn't exactly my taste—really modern with white Formica drawers and a headboard with odd, geometric storage spaces, like something you'd see in a futuristic movie from the 1970s—but beggars can't be choosers, and anyone who's spent eight months sleeping on an air mattress is definitely a beggar. I went back upstairs to thank Mara, but nobody was home.

The next night Mara and the Princesses and I actually ended up having dinner together. I couldn't believe it—were there absolutely no movies they wanted to see?

No stores they had to empty of merchandise? Not a restaurant open on the North Shore at which they could dine without having to tolerate my presence?

But within seconds, it became clear why they didn't mind eating with me—it was because they weren't, really. Mara's *Vogue* had arrived earlier in the day, as had the Princesses' *TeenVogue*. This is something akin to a national holiday here at Casa Norton, and once it had been established that my jeans were "the wrong brand," no one bothered to talk to me. I ate my pasta thinking about a Picasso painting Ms. Daniels had shown me earlier in response to my latest (and lamest) idea for a self-portrait. Called "Large Nude in a Red Armchair," it was a bizarre rendering of a woman whose head and teeth made her look like an angry horse. Ms. Daniels's point was that Picasso painted portraits that were simultaneously of people's exteriors *and* interiors. "What does Lucy's interior self look like?" she kept asking.

Thinking about your interior self and eating pasta isn't exactly appetizing; as I twirled each mouthful onto my fork, I imagined the strands of spaghetti were my intestines. I was getting into the image in spite of its grossness, considering a self-portrait of me eating a plate of my own organs, which may be why I missed my name being called.

"He-*lo*!" Princess One looked at me with exasperation. "Earth to Lucy, Earth to Lucy." She rolled her eyes at her sister.

"Sorry," I said. "Were you talking to me?"

"No, Lucy, I was," said Mara. She reached over and patted my hand, like I was an untrainable puppy she was saddled with.

"Sorry," I said again.

"My friend Gail is coming to New York on Saturday, and I've invited her to stay with us for the week. I was hoping she could stay in your room, and you could stay in the den." She adjusted her bangs and took a sip of wine.

"Wait," I said, and then because I couldn't formulate a thought, I just said, "What?"

Mara gave me her toothpaste-commercial smile, like we were great friends who often asked tiny little favors of each other. "I said I was wondering if you'd be willing to let my friend Gail sleep in your room when she comes on Saturday."

"Why can't Gail stay in the den?" I asked. It seemed pretty strange to me that Mara wasn't housing her friend in our newly color-coordinated den, especially since during the months when she was decorating it, I must have had to listen to her use the phrase "convertible sofa bed" ten thousand times.

"The thing is, she's got a back problem, and I hate to ask her to sleep on a sofa bed." *Or an air mattress.* Suddenly the appearance of my new bed wasn't quite so magical.

I knew I was supposed to feel bad about her friend's

back, but considering she'd barely spoken to me in days, I wasn't exactly dying to do Mara a favor.

"Well," I said, "I'm not sure. Can I think about it?"

Mara's high-wattage smile dimmed. "Of course, Lucy. It's your room."

"God, Lucy, you don't have to be so selfish," said Princess One.

"Yeah," said Princess Two. "Gail was in a *car accident* when she was a kid."

"And yet I don't see you offering up *your* bed," I snapped.

"Okay, Lucy, that's enough," said Mara, choosing to overlook the fact that her daughter had just called me selfish. "If you don't want to help, it's up to you."

"I didn't say I don't want to help," I said. "I just said I want to think about it."

"What's there to think about?" asked Princess Two. "Either you want to help or you don't."

"Some of us like to think," I said, glaring at her. "We don't all think it's a crime to actually use our brains."

Mara hit the table with her palm, making her wineglass jump. "Lucy, I will not have you speak that way to your sister."

"What about how she's talking to me?!" Was Mara *deaf*? Or did she just choose not to hear what came out of her daughters' mouths?

"All I said is that you're being selfish," said Princess

One. "It's not bad to say something if it's true." She turned to her mother. "Isn't that right?"

"I am so *not* selfish," I said. "And I don't exactly see you volunteering your bed for Gail to sleep in."

"I would totally volunteer my bed, but I happen to have a bad back, too," said Princess One.

"Oh, please," I said. "Just because Little Miss Thing likes to sleep in her own bed suddenly she's got back problems?"

Princess One turned to her mother. "Mom, Lucy's being mean to me."

"Talk about being able to dish it out but not take it," I said. "Don't go whining to Mommy, you little brat."

"That's *enough*, Lucy!" said Mara. "When I tell your father that—"

"Oh, sure, bring my father into this." I made my voice high-pitched and whiny. "*Oh, Doug! Doug, darling. Come home quickly. You'll never believe what Lucy's done this time.* Let me get you the phone, Mara. Let me get the phone so you can tell him all about his terrible daughter." This was so typical. I knew she'd never tell him the Princesses had called me selfish and unhelpful. She'd make it sound like they'd been all, *Hey, Lucy, how was your day?* and I'd responded, *None of your business, you selfish brats.*

"I think your father has a right to know how his daughter behaves in his absence," Mara said. Her voice was threatening.

Talk about unfair. I could feel myself starting to cry. I blinked rapidly, trying to hold back the tears. "How about how *they* behave in his absence?" I pointed across the table.

"The way the girls behave is between them and me," said Mara. "I'll discipline them."

"Oh, please," I said. "If you look up discipline in the dictionary, it doesn't say, 'Take shopping for new clothes.'"

Mara threw her napkin down on the table. "I will not be spoken to like that in my house."

"Oh, so now it's your house." There was nothing I could do to stop the tears from running down my cheeks. I pushed my chair back and stood up. "I knew all that stuff about it's being 'our' house was a load of crap."

"How dare you!" hissed Mara, standing up, too. "You go to your room right this minute."

"You're not *sending* me to my room," I said, half sobbing and half yelling. "I'm *choosing* to go there because it's as far away from you as I can get!"

When I got to the basement I tried to slam the door shut, but since it opened out, that wasn't really possible. I had to settle for pulling it closed behind me as hard as I could. I paced around the room, seething. I had never hated anyone as much as I hated Mara. I wished I was the kind of person who could commit a murder and make it look like an accident. I wished I was the kind of person who could commit a murder and *not* make it look like an accident. What did I care if I went to jail? Could life in prison really be that much worse than life with my stepmother?

Finally I collapsed on my bed and tried to calm myself by letting my eyes get lost in Matisse's fluid shapes and colors. It didn't work, though. I just lay there, hating Mara and my stepsisters, until suddenly it occurred to me that I didn't even know the name of my dad's hotel in San Francisco. There was no way for me to call him unless I first went to Mara and got the number. It scared me. What if I wanted to talk to him and she wouldn't let me? And even if I *could* get to him, what if he wouldn't help me?

I put on my headphones and let *whitechocolate-spaceegg* blast my thoughts out of my brain. Sometime later, fully dressed and with the lights still on, I must have fallen asleep.

Chapter Fourteen

I woke up before my alarm went off and lay in my bed for a while, watching the minutes advance from forty-eight to fifty-five. Then I went upstairs to get some orange juice. On the kitchen table was a note in Mara's spindly handwriting.

LUCY, YOUR FATHER AND I EXPECT YOU HOME RIGHT AFTER SCHOOL.

I stood there, reading and rereading the note, like it was in some foreign language in which I wasn't yet fluent.

At eight o'clock, the game that would determine whether or not we made it to the state championship was going to start, and approximately two hours later, Connor and everyone else I knew at Glen Lake would be celebrating at Darren Smith's house. Darren's party was going to be huge. No, not huge. Gigantic. Mind blowing.

Earth shattering.

I'd already missed the second-biggest party of the year because of Mara. No way was I missing the biggest. What were the odds I'd come home from school, have a civilized conversation with my dad and Mara about last night's fight, and then be allowed to go to Darren's party? My parting shot at Mara floated before my eyes, as if the fight had been close-captioned for the memory impaired. IT'S AS FAR AWAY FROM YOU AS I CAN GET!

No one but me was up yet. I went back downstairs, took a three-minute shower, got dressed, "forgot" my cell phone on my bed and threw a mind-blowing, party-worthy outfit into my bag before slipping out the back door. Rather than risk being cornered by Mara's Mercedes at the bus stop, I walked the mile and a half to Glen Lake, arriving at school almost an hour early.

All morning I sat in my classes feeling like a fugitive. Twice someone knocked on the classroom door, once in English and once in chemistry, and handed a note to the teacher. Each time I expected her to look up, catch my eye, and read out loud from the slip of paper, *Lucy Norton, you are grounded for the rest of your life. Pack up your things; the police are waiting for you in the principal's office.* It took me until lunch to realize how stupid I was being. No one was coming to get me, certainly not before three-thirty, when they could reasonably start expecting me home. Once I stopped seeing myself as an escaped convict, the day stretching out before the eight o'clock basketball game started to feel interminable.

What was I going to do between two-fifty, when my last class was over, and game time?

"Hey, what are you doing after school?" I asked Madison.

"Doctor's appointment," she said, breaking off a piece of my chocolate-chip cookie and popping it in her mouth.

Jessica wasn't allowed to go to the game unless she went straight home from school and worked on a history paper. In the space of ten minutes, I went from having two viable after-school options to having none. Though maybe hanging out at Jessica's or Madison's wouldn't have been such a good idea anyway; that was the first place Mara would look for me once it became clear I'd disobeyed her.

When last period ended, I stayed at my easel while everyone else packed up. Since I didn't have anyplace else to go, I figured I might as well try putting the time to good use. The class slowly filed out, leaving me alone with my sketches. The problem was I still didn't really understand what Ms. Daniels wanted from us. Now I stood facing yet another blank sheet of paper and chewing on my eraser, trying to decide if it was morally suspect to open other people's drawers and steal their ideas. When the door to the studio opened, I looked up. Maybe it was Connor; I'd called his cell from the pay phone by the gym to see if he wanted to go for a drive before the game. By "go for a drive," I meant "make out," the only activity in the universe that could possibly have gotten my mind off my deeply troubled home life.

It wasn't Connor, it was Andrea, this totally annoying girl who's in Ms. Daniels's figure-drawing class. When no one's in the studio, she likes to come in here and talk on her cell. She looked at me, decided I was no one, and reached into her bag. Then she went over to the sofa, threw herself down, and dialed a number on her phone.

"*Hel-lo!* No, it's me. . . . Oh my god. . . . Really?" Her piercing voice could have cut glass. "They *did*? . . . But I *told* you. . . . No *I* told you that . . ." I packed my stuff up as fast as I could and stuffed it into my drawer. In a moment of perfect symmetry, just as the studio door closed behind me, I heard Andrea say, "Get *out!*"

The hallway was deserted. Three twenty-five. Four hours and thirty-five minutes till game time. Maybe I'd call a taxi and go to Barnes and Noble and do homework. I made my way to my locker. Should I go to a movie? But who goes to a movie all by herself in the middle of the afternoon? I wished I could just be cryogenically frozen for a few hours and then emerge, well-rested, if slightly chilly, in time for the tip-off.

There was something on my locker. From a distance it looked like a newspaper clipping, but as I got closer I realized it was a postcard. I studied the front of the card, which was a photo of a painting, a portrait. Then I turned the card over. MILTON NEWMAN: NEW WORKS. THE MARGARET TANNER GALLERY. 525 WEST FOURTEENTH

STREET. NEW YORK CITY. OPENING RECEPTION MARCH 31. FIVE TO SEVEN.

March 31st—that was today. I looked around, totally freaked out. This was way too big a coincidence. Who knew me well enough to know I A) liked art and B) had four hours to kill? Connor? No, he probably hadn't even gotten my message. Madison? She was hardly a player on the New York art scene. Jessica? Ditto. No. No. No. Was someone watching me? Had someone overheard me asking Jessica and Madison if we could hang out after school? Did I have some kind of freak stalker situation on my hands?

Just as I was starting to get totally weirded out about being all alone in the hallway with a potential stalker, the answer came to me. Ms. Daniels. Of course. She must have stuck the card on my locker. All the teachers have a list of student locker assignments, so if they get the urge they can order a student's locker be searched for drugs or porn or credit card receipts from termpaper.com.

But wouldn't Ms. Daniels have given me the post-card in class? Or told me about the opening like she had the Clemente exhibit? The whole thing was really strange. Then again, my locker was between the studio and the faculty parking lot. Maybe she'd meant to give it to me in class but then forgotten. I could totally picture Ms. Daniels walking along the hall, reaching into her bag for her car keys, and finding the card in her bag. She probably carried the locker numbers in her briefcase with her roll book or something. It made total sense.

I'd never heard of Milton Newman before, but the portrait was fantastically cool, almost but not quite photo-realistic. It reminded me a tiny bit of something I'd seen before, but I couldn't think of what. I checked the hall clock. Three-thirty. It was only a five-minute taxi ride to the Glen Lake train station. The opening was from five to eight. I could go into the city, see the paintings, and be back on Long Island in plenty of time for the game.

I'd just been invited to my first New York art opening. For the second time this year, Ms. Daniels had singled me out from the rest of the class as someone who would benefit from seeing an exhibit she liked. Was I really going to say no?

Luckily the change of clothes I'd brought for the party could double as Manhattan gallery–opening wear: chunky-heeled black boots, black low-rider pants, and a tiny, paper thin, pale blue C and C T-shirt Madison had given me last week, since she said it looked really cute on me and she never wore it anymore. I could change, go into the city, see the paintings, mix and mingle, then hop on the train and be back in Glen Lake with plenty of time before the game started.

My afternoon had suddenly gone from sucky to stupendous.

I'd have to remember to tell Ms. Daniels she made an excellent fairy godmother.

Chapter Fifteen

When my cab pulled up in front of the Margaret Tanner gallery just after five, the sun was hanging low over the Hudson River, and the entire block exploded with light. The gallery sat on a lawn of white gravel, slightly apart from the neighboring buildings, and there was a small reflecting pool out front. A rough-hewn stone wall ran around the property.

The front of the gallery was all glass, and through it I could see the crowd and some of the paintings: enormous, photo-realistic portraits. As I stood at the gate, looking across the gravel lawn, a taxi pulled up and a couple emerged, chatting in Italian. The woman had short, spiky hair and the man wore tiny, geometric glasses; they were both thin and chic, and as they walked past the reflecting pool, they looked like something out of a *Vogue* photo spread.

Clearly it was a very good thing I was wearing black pants.

Inside, the crowd was equally fabulous. The women, even the older ones, were tanned and toned, and a lot of them were wearing microminis. The men wore linen suits or expensive-looking shirt-pant combinations that even someone as fashion impaired as the Princesses insist I am could tell were extremely hip. The well-lit room buzzed, and the occasional pop of a flash camera only added to the feeling that this was an important celebrity gathering.

The artist, whom I recognized from the postcard (apparently a self-portrait), was standing over in one corner, surrounded by a mob of people. I headed for two of the paintings I hadn't seen from the street. These were enormous landscapes, so rich and varied my eyes felt overwhelmed, and I realized who Newman's work reminded me of—Chuck Close. I circled in front of one of the paintings slowly, watching the swirls and lines seem to change color as I looked at them from different angels. Painting was just so *cool*. How did people know how to do that, to put colors and shapes next to each other in just the right pattern? I wondered if my mother could have explained it to me, or if it was all intuitive, impossible to articulate.

I stepped back from the painting, looking around the room for Ms. Daniels. The truth was I couldn't quite picture her in this crowd. Perhaps she transformed into super-hip, Manhattan-art-scene woman as soon as school was out. I scrutinized a few of the microminied women more closely, ultimately determining that the only way Ms. Daniels was in the room with me was if she'd chopped off her long hair and dyed it platinum blond, cherry-red, or blue.

I figured I'd find her before I left; maybe she was one of those people who believed in arriving fashionably late. Plus, I was starting to feel self-conscious standing in the corner looking around the room for a familiar face. I turned back to look at a painting I'd been studying, but unfortunately right then I *did* see a familiar face. Only it wasn't the familiar face I wanted to see. It was someone else from my class whom Ms. Daniels must have invited.

Sam Wolff.

Ugh.

Sam was half turned away from me. He was wearing a sports jacket and a pair of charcoal flannel pants, and he was talking to the artist, who said something that made Sam throw his head back and laugh. I couldn't believe it. Why did my first New York opening have to include Sam Wolff? And why did Sam have to be standing there, casually chatting with the artist like they were best buddies? I could already see how he'd act when he saw I was at the opening, too. He'd either A) totally ignore me or B) seek me out in order to say something condescending. God, why was he such a jerk? It was enough to make me want to leave without even bothering to see the rest of the paintings.

I was about to zip up my jacket and head out, when I realized how stupid I was being. I mean, I had just as much right to be here as he did. It wasn't like he owned the place. Who cared if he was sucking up to the artist while I was standing alone in the corner? Ms. Daniels had invited *both* of us. I'd look at the paintings, thank her for inviting me, and leave. There was no reason I even had to say hello to him.

Just as I was turning my back to where he was standing, Sam looked over in my direction. Great. I saw him excuse himself, and he came toward me.

"So, you decided to brave the streets of Gotham." His cheeks were flushed, and he held a half-empty wineglass in one hand. He touched the sleeve of my jacket. "Did you, in fact, bring the football team with you?"

"Basketball," I corrected him, pulling my arm away from his hand. "I hate football."

"Oh, sorry," he said. "I didn't realize there was a difference."

This was too much. "You didn't *realize* there was a difference?" Crossing my arms, I gave a sarcastic laugh. "Oh, please. You think it makes you seem all 'intellectual' and 'artistic' to say, 'My goodness, there's a difference between football and basketball? How quaint.' But it doesn't make you sound smart, it makes you sound like an idiot. Like a person who doesn't know there's a difference between Picasso and Monet."

Even as the words were coming out of my mouth, I

couldn't believe how obnoxious I was being. I never talked this way to anyone. Not even my stepmother.

"Wow, that's an impressive analogy," he said. "Football is to basketball as Picasso is to Monet." A waiter passed by with a tray of wineglasses, and Sam took one and handed it to me.

I took it, but I didn't thank him. Just because Ms. Daniels happened to have invited the two of us to the same opening didn't mean I had to be polite to him. I wished I could find her, though. It was getting increasingly weird to be at a party without the person who invited me.

Sam poked my shoulder with his index finger. "So, what, if I don't care about the finer points of basketball, you're not going to talk to me?"

I wanted to tell him not to poke me. I also wanted to tell him I wasn't going to talk to him even if he *did* care about the finer points of basketball, but just as I opened my mouth to say those things, Sam looked across the room at a man and a woman who were making a beeline in our direction. "Oh, Jesus," he muttered. He took a swallow of wine and centered himself over his feet as if bracing for some sort of attack. For a second I thought I saw something in his face I'd never seen before—something a little sad or maybe confused. And then, just as quickly as it had appeared, it was gone.

"Darling," said the woman, swooping down on us. "I want you to meet Diego Martinez. Diego, this is my son, Sam. He's an artist as well." She put her arm around Sam and air kissed his cheek.

This night was getting weirder and weirder. What was Sam's mom doing here?

"Nice to meet you," said Sam, holding out his hand for Diego to shake.

Diego was wearing a perfectly wrinkled black suit. "Charmed," he said. I didn't recognize his name, but Diego Martinez's suit, along with his five-o'clock shadow, made him look exactly how an artist *should* look.

"And this is?" Sam's mother was looking at me inquiringly. She had on a pale green silk tank top and black silk palazzo pants, and her chin-length dyed hair was way redder than mine.

"Lucy Norton, Maggie Tanner," said Sam. "Mom, Lucy."

Tanner. Her name was very familiar. Where had I heard it before?

"Of course. Lucy." She waved her arm around the room. "So, how do you like my little show?" she asked.

Oh my god. Oh my god. OHMYGOD.

Suddenly I remembered where I'd seen the name Margaret Tanner.

"Oh, ah, it's great," I said. "It's really a great show."

This was *her* gallery. Which meant—

"Yes, Sam thought you'd enjoy it," she said. She took Diego by the arm. "And just wait until you see what *this* genius can do."

Sam had invited me? Sam?!

"Of course," I said. "I, um, look forward to it."

Diego smiled, took Sam's mom's hand, and kissed each of the fingers, one at a time. The process seemed to take forever. "With Maggie at my side, I am unstoppable," he said finally. "Have you ever seen a more beautiful gallery owner in your life?"

Apparently this was a rhetorical question because Sam's mom just said, "Darling," and beamed at us before giving a little wave. "Well, we're off. Enjoy."

"Thanks," I said. I watched them walk a few steps before Sam's mom was embraced by a tall man with a goatee. I heard her say, *"Darling!"*

"You know what?" Sam asked, looking not at me but at a spot just over my shoulder.

I shook my head. "What?"

"I need to get some air."

I wasn't sure if he meant for me to follow, but I did.

"Thanks for inviting me," I said, wincing inwardly at the memory of how rude I'd been to him earlier. We were sitting outside on a bench a few feet from the reflecting pool. Sam hadn't said anything since we'd gotten outside, and my sentence came out awkward and rehearsed, which made sense, considering I'd experimented with several variations of it in my head before uttering it.

"Yeah, sure," he said, but he sounded distracted, like he hadn't really heard what I'd said.

I figured I might as well get the whole thing over with all at once. "I, um, didn't realize you'd put the card on my locker," I said. "I thought Ms. Daniels invited me."

Sam stood up and walked over to the reflecting pool. "Oh." He said. He leaped up onto the stone wall that ran around the pool and started walking along it. "Disappointed?"

"What?"

"I said, are you disappointed?"

Now I was confused. "About what?"

"That I'm the one who invited you?"

"No. Why would I be disappointed?"

He was walking totally naturally, even though the stone lip he was balanced on was only a couple of inches wide. "I don't know. Why would you assume Ms. Daniels was the one who had invited you? Why wouldn't you think it could be me?"

"Ah, maybe because every time I try to talk to you, you look at me like you wish I'd get hit by a car," I answered.

"Come on," he said, from the other side of the pool.

"Or a bus."

"Please. I'm not *that* bad. It's just . . . embarrassing when someone comments on your painting."

I thought about explaining the difference between a comment and a compliment, but from the way he was suddenly looking down, I could tell just talking about my talking about his artwork was making him uncomfortable.

"How did you know which one was my locker?" I asked.

"Your notebook."

"What?"

"It's on your notebook."

"Oh," It was true. The first day of school I'd written my locker number on my notebook so I wouldn't forget it.

Sam was two thirds of the way around the pool now, and he looked over at me. Then he jumped off without even spilling a drop of his wine and came back to the bench. He stood in front of where I was sitting and ran his hand through his hair, making it stand up straight. Then he shook his head like he was trying to clear it of something unpleasant. "Sorry about my mother back there," he said.

"Don't worry about it," I said. "You should meet my stepmother."

"Yeah?" he asked.

"God yes, she's ten million times worse than your mom." I thought for a second. "Like, she collects really expensive glass figurines," I said.

"No way!" Sam said, and for the first time since his mom had come over to us, he smiled.

"Really," I said. "And once one of a pair of matching unicorns broke, and she started to *cry*." Sam was still smiling. "At least your mom collects art," I said.

"And artists," he said. He stopped smiling and looked back at the gallery. "What about your mother?" he asked. "What does she do?"

"Actually, she doesn't do anything anymore," I said. "She's dead."

"Oh, wow," he said, turning back to face me. "That sucks."

"Yeah, I guess," I said. I never know how to tell people my mother's dead, since it's pretty much guaranteed to bring even the most scintillating conversation to a complete halt. It was a huge relief that Sam hadn't made the *Poor little Lucy* frown most people made.

"Is that why you moved to New York?" he asked. "Did she die recently?"

"Oh, no, she died a long time ago," I said. "We moved because my dad remarried, and my revolting stepsisters can't function outside a ten-mile radius of the Miracle Mile."

Sam squinted and looked up at the sky, like he was trying to figure something out. "Soooo, you've got a stepmother who's a bitch and some evil stepsisters," he said finally.

"I know," I said. "It's so Brothers Grimm."

"Seriously."

As I looked at Sam, who was standing right in front of me and still looking up at the sky, I could kind of see why someone like Jane, someone who could go out with any guy she wanted to, might go out with him. In his sports jacket, holding a glass of wine, he looked good. Not good like Connor looked good. Not in the pure gorgeous way. This was different. I considered how Sam had laughed when he was talking to Milton Newman. Even though there must have been at least a dozen adults around him, even though he was talking to a guy who was clearly a successful, well-known artist, he'd seemed totally relaxed.

That was it—Sam was cool.

He sat down on the bench next to me. "So," he said. "You're uprooted from San Francisco and dragged across the country to Long Island. You're a sophomore. You know no one. Yet in just a few short months you manage to snag the captain of the football—sorry, the *basketball* team. Not too shabby."

I took a sip of my wine, then turned to face him. "I really don't think the guy who went out with last year's prom queen ought to be quite so condescending, do you?"

Sam laughed. "Touché," he said. After a minute he added, "She wasn't *actually* the prom queen."

"Still," I said, patting him lightly on the knee. "I feel the point is justified."

"Yeah," he acknowledged. "I suppose it is." He stretched his arms up, then dropped his hands onto his head and ran his fingers through his hair. "Hey, maybe *you'll* get to be prom queen this year," he said. Then he pointed at me. "Dreams come true, right?"

I put my glass down on the pebbled ground. "Okay, can I just say that I didn't like you before, and then for a few minutes I liked you, and now I'm not liking you again?"

"Sorry," he said. When I didn't say anything, he said it again. "Really, I'm sorry." He shook his head and chuckled. "I just *cannot* understand how someone who seems to care about art as much as you do cares about basketball."

I crossed my arms. "Why not? Why can't you accept that a person could like sports *and* art?"

"I don't know." He shrugged. "Failure of imagination, I guess."

"Failure of something," I said. "You should care about basketball. You should open your mind to the beauty of the game."

Sam shook his head from side to side, smiling. "Well, maybe I'll do that," he said.

"Speaking of the beauty of the game, what time is it?" I asked. I was pretty sure it was getting close to seven, which meant I needed to think about leaving. There was a seven-twenty train I planned to be on, and Penn Station was about ten minutes from the gallery by cab.

Sam reached over and lazily pushed up the sleeve of his jacket. "It's seven-ten," he said.

I leaped up off the bench, my heart pounding. "Oh my god! How is that possible?"

157

"Well, the big hand's on the—"

"No, no, I have to get out of here," I said. "I'm late."

He scrunched up his face in mock confusion. "Wait, let me guess . . ." Suddenly he waved his hand in the air. "I know, I know. It must be the night of the BIG GAME, right?"

I couldn't help smiling. "If I had the time, I'd punch you," I said.

"In that case, I'd better get you a cab," he said, and he turned and walked toward the gate. I followed and waited on the sidewalk while he hailed a cab, trying not to tap my foot impatiently. Luckily a cab pulled up right away; within a minute Sam was holding the door open for me.

As I slid into the backseat, it occurred to me how rude I was being. "Sorry to race off like this," I said, buckling my seat belt.

"No worries," he said. "I wouldn't want you to turn into a pumpkin right before my eyes." And then, smiling, he shut the door of the cab.

"Where to?" asked the driver.

"Penn Station, please." The cab sped off, and when we stopped at the corner for a light, I realized I hadn't even really said good-bye. I craned my neck around to see if Sam was still standing outside the gallery, but he wasn't there. I leaned back against the seat.

"Do you know what time it is?" I asked the driver.

"It's seven-fifteen," he said.

If I missed the seven-twenty train, the next one was the seven-forty, which meant there was no way I'd get to the eight o'clock game before eight-thirty.

It was all Mara's fault. If she hadn't been such a witch, we wouldn't have gotten into a fight, and if we hadn't gotten into a fight, I wouldn't have had to come to the city to avoid getting grounded, and if I hadn't had to come to the city to avoid getting grounded, I wouldn't have stayed at the gallery all that time talking to Sam, and if I hadn't stayed at the gallery talking to Sam, I wouldn't have missed my train, and if I hadn't missed my train, I wouldn't be late to the game.

Tonight was a perfect illustration of why Cinderella and the Prince get married twenty-four hours after they meet. Because when you're living with your stepmother, there *is* no happily ever after.

Chapter Sixteen

I'd expected to arrive halfway through the first quarter if I was lucky, but when I yanked open the door of the gym, the teams were still warming up. How was that possible? Looking up at the clock just under the scoreboard, I saw that it said eight-thirty. So I *was* late. But so was the game.

I stood by the door watching as each player took a shot and then melted into the snaking line of players forming and reforming below the basket. Fans cheered so wildly the gym literally shook. Music blared out of the loudspeakers, and the room itself seemed to be sweating from all the bodies crammed inside. I felt the heat and noise acting on me like an elixir. In less than a minute I'd identified Connor—like magic, the second I saw him, he sank a perfect layup, and the crowd, me included, went wild.

It took forever to find Madison and Jessica, and then my chunky-heeled boots turned the climb up to were they were sitting into an aerobics class. By the time I arrived at the sliver of space they'd been able to save for me, I was panting as hard as the guys on the team. "Sorry I'm late," I said after I'd hugged them both hello. Then I looked down at the court just in time to see us lose the tip.

Jessica waved away my apology. "Guess what?" she asked.

South Meadow was good. Really good. We'd barely managed to get the ball when they got it back.

"Know what?" Jessica asked again.

I pointed at the clock. "Why'd the game start late?"

"I think their bus broke down or something," Madison said. I watched as the ref called Glen Lake for traveling.

"Aren't you going to ask what?" said Jessica.

"What what?" I asked. South Meadow made the foul shot, and I managed to take my eyes off the court long enough to notice both Madison and Jessica were grinning from ear to ear. "What?" I repeated.

"The prom committee's announcing the prom theme on Monday." Her smile broadened. "And you know what else?"

"What?" The ref blew his whistle just as Jessica put her arm around my shoulder and leaned in to whisper in my ear. Had he called *another* foul against Glen Lake? I couldn't see. "What three girls are the only sophomores who will be receiving invitations?"

Suddenly my mind was very much not on the game. "No!" I said, staring at her.

Jessica nodded. "Yes."

Now I started to smile, too. "Wait a sec," I said, rethinking what she'd said. "You don't *know* they're going to ask us."

Madison put her arm around my other shoulder and leaned into me, the three of us forming a tight huddle. "Not only are they going to ask us," she said, "but I think they're going to ask us *tonight*."

"Tonight?" I repeated.

She and Jessica squeezed me, like they were making a Lucy sandwich. "Tonight," said Jessica.

Just then Connor got the ball, and the three of us leaped to our feet along with the rest of the Glen Lake fans. I cheered until I was hoarse as Connor dribbled the ball toward the net, moving so easily he didn't even need to fake out the people sent to guard him—his fluid body simply swayed one way, then another, and suddenly there was only empty space where he'd been a second before. Watching him sink the ball, I couldn't believe someone so confident and talented had chosen *me* to be his girlfriend.

Still clapping, Jessica leaned into me. "There goes your prom date," she said.

"Stop," I said, hitting her on the shoulder. "Watch

the game." But I couldn't help laughing and neither could she.

It was probably the only time anyone on our side of the gym laughed all night. By the third quarter, the game, which everyone had predicted would be a close one, was proving to be anything but. South Meadow—a team that seemed to have the ability to read one another's minds, twelve giants who dwarfed even our tallest players—was unbeatable. No, not unbeatable—untouchable. While they sank basket after basket, we barely scored, until eventually we were behind by almost thirty points. Their coach started rotating in players who probably hadn't been off the bench all season, letting the score get a little closer before sending back in a well-rested starter or two. Our starters, meanwhile, were exhausted; they'd been running all night, but the few times they were rotated out they couldn't sit still. I watched them pace back and forth along the court, swigging water restlessly until they were sent back in. When the final buzzer rang and South Meadow had won by fifteen, most of the guys on the Glen Lake bench were holding their heads in their hands. A few were actually crying.

Even Madison and Jessica were crushed, though for a very different reason. "The guys are gonna be so pissed," said Madison.

"Maybe we should go to the diner for a while," suggested Jessica. "You know, give them a chance to wallow a little?"

We decided that was a good idea, and while Madison called a cab to take us to Dan's Diner, Jessica text-messaged Dave that we'd meet them at the party. When I took out my wallet to check how much cash I had, I saw a corner of the postcard Sam had put on my locker. In the midst of being so depressed, it was nice to remember the part of the evening that hadn't been a complete disaster.

We didn't talk much at Dan's, and nobody uttered the word *prom*. We just sat over our fries and Cokes, wondering how disappointed the guys were going to be, until finally Jessica decided we'd waited long enough and she called a cab to take us to the no-victory party.

Even though I knew Connor was going to be totally bummed about losing, my heart couldn't stop doing its little tap dance of excitement the whole ride. This was going to be my first official high-school party. And it wasn't like I was going as some desperate, dorky freshman or even an anonymous sophomore—I was going as Connor Pearson's girlfriend. Maybe the basketball team was suffering the agony of defeat, but I couldn't help feeling the thrill of victory.

We turned off Cypress Avenue and started making our way through what was clearly a mega-rich neighborhood, the kind where you can't even see the houses from the road. As we got closer to Darren's, traffic suddenly became a problem—cars were parked on both sides of the street, and our cab slowed to a crawl to make its way between the rows. We pulled up in front of a gigantic wrought-iron gate with an iron eagle perched on top of it, paid the driver, and joined the river of people heading up the gravel driveway. Hovering on a rise above us was Darren's house, the biggest home I'd ever seen outside of a movie set; it was as if a French Chateau had been lifted off its foundation, flown across the Atlantic Ocean, and dropped, perfectly intact, onto the North Shore of Long Island.

Inside the massive front door a group of guys was playing Nerf basketball; the foyer was so big their game wasn't even disturbed by the crowds of people milling around. Madison, Jessica, and I looked at each other. The entryway branched off in two directions, and Jessica held her hands out like a pair of scales, standing like that until Madison tapped her right arm. We turned right, passed a wide staircase, and headed down a long hallway packed with people. Everyone was drinking something— beer, wine, tropical-looking drinks with frothy heads. We passed Kathryn Ford, Jane Brown, and a bunch of other senior girls drinking champagne right out of the bottle. The house reeked of alcohol and pot; my whole body tingled with excitement.

Okay, true, we'd lost the game. And the season was over. And the seniors, some of whom would probably never play basketball again, had just suffered the worst defeat of their entire careers. But this was the biggest party of the year. Practically the entire school was here. And for the first time since we'd started dating, Connor didn't have a curfew. My head spun with the possibilities. Disobeying Mara's note was, without a doubt, the smartest move I'd made in my entire life.

I couldn't wait to find Connor.

A couple of people we passed said they'd last seen Connor, Matt, and Dave in the kitchen. We kept going, following their instructions. There must have been a hundred rooms in the house. Maybe a thousand. Every time we thought we'd made it to the kitchen, we found ourselves in another library, sitting room, billiard room, conservatory. I was starting to get the feeling the kitchen was like Brigadoon—we could look for it all we wanted, but we'd never find it.

Miles from the front door, we came to a small alcove with nothing in it but a love seat and, spotlighted on the opposite wall, a tiny oil painting in an elaborate gilt frame. As we walked by, I glanced at the painting.

"Oh my god," I said.

"What?" asked Jessica.

"Are you okay?" asked Madison.

I pointed at the young girl in a tutu at a ballet barre. "That's a Degas," I said.

"A what?" asked Madison.

"A Degas. He's this really famous French Impressionist. My dad *loves* him." I shook my head in amazement. "I can't believe they own a Degas."

Madison and Jessica stepped closer to the frame. "Is it, like, superexpensive?" asked Jessica.

"Probably," I said.

Jessica shrugged. "Cool," she said, turning away. "Come on."

We knew we had to be getting close when we heard the chanting. "Go! Go! Go! Go!" Following the noise finally got us to a huge, modern kitchen, bright as an operating room and filled with stainless steel appliances that reflected the scene back on itself, like mirrors in a fun house.

The chanting came from a group of people huddled around a keg in the middle of the room. Dripping wet, with sweat or beer I couldn't tell, Dave was bent over backward at the waist, sucking from a tap. His face was red and the veins on his neck stuck out. Someone was shouting out numbers, and when the person got to thirty, Dave spit out the tap, spraying himself and the people nearby with a mist of beer. Everyone cheered. I didn't see Connor anywhere.

Dave staggered away from the group and collapsed in a chair. The person whose turn it was next grabbed the tap. "Go, Brewster," someone shouted. "Brewster the Brewmeister!" yelled someone else. I watched Jessica, who looked pissed, make her way over to Dave. Madison and I made eye contact. She shrugged and followed Jessica, so I followed her.

Dave had stopped gasping for breath and was laughing at, as far as I could tell, nothing. Jessica, her arms folded tightly across her chest, was shaking her head at him. He stopped laughing and started swaying back and forth in the chair, eyes half closed. "You're wasted, you know that?" she asked, kicking him in the foot.

"I'm notho wasted," he slurred, smiling up at her. "Comeere." He lifted his arms to embrace her and then dropped them, like they were too heavy to hold up. "Okay, maybe wasted."

"Yeah, maybe," she said.

As if to nod in agreement, Dave dropped his head. But it didn't come up again. Once more, Jessica kicked him in the foot. This time all he did was shrug.

"Where's Connor?" I asked. Dave looked up at me, his head swaying. He said something that sounded like, "Background."

"Background?" I repeated.

He took a deep breath and stared into my eyes, all his powers of concentration focused on this elusive communication. "Back. Yard," he managed to say, articulating each syllable with remarkable precision. Then he half pointed, half waved to a corridor that branched off the kitchen and laughed.

"Where's Matt?" asked Madison.

Dave moved his glassy stare from me to Madison and then back again. "Strange," he said.

"What?" she asked.

You could see him gathering himself up for one last push. "Same," he said finally.

She looked at me, confused. "I think he means they're in the same place," I translated.

I started off in the direction Dave had indicated, with Madison right behind me. Jessica gave Dave one more kick in the foot before she followed.

I was starting to get the very bad feeling that my dream night wasn't going quite as I'd planned. We made our way down a long hallway that ended in French doors, which opened onto a deck overlooking the covered swimming pool.

On the deck, passed out under a large glass table, was Connor. A few feet away lay Matt.

Connor was on his stomach with his head resting on his forearm. For a second I wondered if he was still breathing, but then Jessica walked over and kicked his ankle and he groaned.

I bent down. "Connor?" I asked.

"Hey, Red," he said. His words were slurred; I sensed more than heard what he was saying. Then he lifted his head. "Wassup?"

"You okay, Connor?" I sat down on the cold wood and touched his hair. Next to his hip lay an empty bottle of Wild Turkey.

"We lost, Red," said Connor.

"I know," I said. "I'm really sorry."

"I think I need to sleep for a little while," he said, dropping his head back down. "Thanks for stopping by."

Chapter Seventeen

You know what Prince Charming isn't supposed to do? He isn't supposed to puke all over Cinderella's boots. I cleaned Connor's vomit off the leather, helped him climb into Kathryn Ford's car, and sat behind him while he slept, snoring heavily, but I wasn't finding him as charming as I usually did. In fact, I wasn't finding him charming at all.

My father was going to *kill* me. And for what? By the time Kathryn turned onto my block, I was in a panic. My palms were so sweaty I could smell them. For the first time since I'd decided to do it, ignoring Mara's note was starting to feel like a very, very bad idea.

Just as Kathryn pulled up in front of my house, I had a momentary reprieve—it looked as if the only lights on inside were the ones Mara and my dad leave on when they go out for the evening. But then I saw that a lamp was on in my dad's study, and I knew wherever everyone else was, he was home.

And he was waiting for me.

I took a deep breath. "Well, thanks again," I said to Kathryn. "Sorry if this ruined your night."

"Don't worry about it. I told Mark I'd meet up with him in the city." Kathryn's tone made it clear she didn't spend her Friday nights partying with the under twenty one set.

"Oh, right," I said. "You did mention that."

She nodded toward Connor, asleep in the passenger seat. "Our boy's pretty wrecked, isn't he?"

Something about how she said *our* boy kind of rubbed me the wrong way, but it wasn't like I was about to correct her. *Um, actually, Kathryn, he's my boy.*

"Yeah," I said.

She looked at him for a long minute. "He's such a cutie," she said.

Now I was officially irked. *Do not call my boyfriend a cutie.* The hatred I'd reserved for Mara ebbed a bit in the face of my new yet surprisingly powerful hatred for Kathryn Ford.

She clicked her tongue against the roof of her mouth. "Too bad he's too young for me," she said. She turned her head back to where I was sitting, reached through the front seats, and patted my knee. "He's all yours."

"Oh. Ah, thanks," I said. Then I felt like a total idiot

for saying it, since I'd pretty much just thanked her for insulting me. "Well, good night," I said. "Have fun in the city."

"I will," she said.

I went up the front walk as slowly as if I were wearing shoes of lead, literally dragging my heels along the flagstone. In the front hallway, I spent several long minutes taking off Connor's jacket and hanging it up. As soon as I'd shut the closet door, I felt bereft, like the jacket was a suit of armor without which I was totally exposed. For a split second I considered just going downstairs and getting into bed, pretending I hadn't seen my dad's light. But then I thought about how it would feel to defend myself to him in the morning, in front of Mara and the Princesses. As bad as tonight was going to be, tomorrow could only be worse.

I walked through the darkened living room and down the two steps to his study, where a small crack of light glowed under the closed door. I stood there, breathing deeply, and then I knocked.

"Come in," called my dad. I pushed open the door. He was sitting at his desk, typing on his laptop.

"Hey," I said.

"Hey," he said.

"When did you get home?" I asked. I was amazed I was able to keep my voice normal when everything else about me was shaking hard enough for me to feel it.

"A few hours ago," he said. He leaned back in his

chair and put his feet up on the desk, gesturing for me to sit down in the chair facing him. "I heard you had quite a week."

I shrugged and took a seat, feeling like I was settling into the witness stand. "I guess you could say that."

"Want to tell me what happened?" he asked, pushing his hand through his hair.

My dad's not just a lawyer, he's a lawyer who's obsessed with the "inherent beauty" of the American legal system. *Imagine it, Lucy, a country where the accused is innocent until proven guilty.* Usually when he starts waxing rhapsodic about the Bill of Rights, I just roll my eyes or point out that there's nothing especially beautiful about helping multinational corporations sue each other, which is the kind of law my dad practices; but tonight I was glad he was so passionately committed to the rights of the accused. After all, even if Long Island seems like it's in a different universe from San Francisco, officially we were still in the United States.

I sat forward with my hands on my knees. "Okay, the thing is, I didn't do anything, and all of a sudden Mara and everyone was saying how I was being selfish."

"And why do you think they would say a thing like that?" he asked, tapping the tips of his fingers together.

I was totally relieved. I'd thought he was automatically going to take Mara's side, but now I could see he was going to listen to my version of the story. "I don't *know*," I said. "Mara asked me to let her friend sleep in my room, and I asked her if I could think about it, and all of a sudden everyone was acting like I'd said no, when I hadn't."

"So you feel you were ganged up on for *no reason at all*?" Was it my imagination, or had his tone changed? Before he had sounded genuinely curious; now he sounded overly curious, i.e., like he really wasn't curious at all.

I refused to believe my dad's question was rhetorical. Was it really *that* impossible for him to imagine his precious wife and stepdaughters might possibly gang up on his innocent daughter. "As a matter of fact, I *do* think that."

"Well, I wasn't there, Lucy, so I can't say for sure what happened, but Mara made it sound like you were inexcusably rude to her for absolutely no reason."

"Well, did it ever occur to you that just because Mara made it *sound* like that doesn't mean it *happened* like that?"

"Lucy, I don't understand what's going on here." He dropped his feet to the floor and sat forward in his chair. "Mara said she asked you to do her friend Gail a favor, and you said no, and then you started shouting at her and the girls." He wasn't yelling, but I could tell he was getting frustrated.

"I can't believe you're just taking her side like that," I said. "You're not even listening to me."

"Lucy, I am *not* taking sides. I'm only telling you what I heard."

But when he put his hands flat on the desk's green blotter, his wedding ring gleamed.

I gripped the arms of my chair, hard. "Well, you heard wrong."

"So what *did* happen?"

Had he totally missed my previous description?

Even though I've never been much of a crier, for the second time in as many days, I felt my chin quiver and my eyes filling with tears. "You don't understand what it's like for me living here. You're off in San Francisco living it up while I'm trapped with the Wicked Witch of the East and her evil spawn."

As soon as the words were out of my mouth, I regretted them. Some things aren't meant to be said out loud.

My dad put his face in his hands and rubbed his eyes. Then he looked up at me. "Lucy, when you say things like that, it makes it *really* hard for me to believe Mara's making up stories about how you insult her and the girls."

I snorted. "Oh, yeah, like you'd believe me even if I *didn't* say things like that."

"Why do you act like we're all ganged up against you? Everyone is struggling to make this family work. Everyone."

I couldn't believe it. *Struggling? Struggling!* "Do you mean *shopping*, Dad? Do you mean everyone is *shopping* to make this family work? Because I don't see a whole lot of *struggling* going on around here."

"And that is *exactly* the kind of snotty response I'm tired of," said my dad. "How is that a helpful thing to say?"

"Well, maybe I don't *want* to be helpful," I said, standing up. "Maybe I'm tired of being helpful."

My dad stood up, too. "Tired of being helpful? Lucy, to be tired of something you have to do it for a while."

"You know they totally ignore me when you're not here, Dad. All they do is go shopping and go to movies and go to dinner *without* me."

"Lucy, just last weekend Mara asked you to come into the city with us, and you said no."

"Dad, are you *blind*? She only asked me to go because you were sitting right there. She wants you to think she cares about me, but really, she hates me."

"She hates you? Is that why she was so upset that you yelled at her last night, because she hates you? If she hated you, would she even care? Would she even care that you don't come home when she tells you to? Wouldn't she be just as happy not to see you if she hated you?"

"No," I said, sniffling. "She doesn't just hate me. She hates me *and* she wants to ruin my life."

"Lucy, I really don't know how you expect me to respond to that kind of paranoia."

He didn't say anything after that, and I didn't either. I knew it was pointless for me to try and defend myself anymore.

We were now moving on to the sentencing phase of the trial.

"I want you to apologize to Mara for what happened," he said. He took some tissues out of the box on his desk and handed them to me. "I know it would mean a lot to her after what you said. And until we see a real change in your behavior, you're not to go out with your friends."

I'd had my nose buried in a tissue, but when he said that last part, my head snapped up. "Grounded? You're *grounding* me? For how long?" As far as I could tell, he'd just grounded me indefinitely.

"Until we see a change in your attitude." He waited a second, but I was too nonplussed by my punishment to respond. Finally he continued. "Look, I know you're sad, Lucy, and I'm sorry. But I think if you think about it, you'll see you're bringing this on yourself."

The room was deadly silent. When it became clear I still wasn't going to say anything, my dad sat down. I stayed standing, and he looked up at me. "Why don't you get some sleep, Goose. If you want, we can talk about this in the morning. Good night."

He didn't even wait for me to leave the room before turning back to his computer. I had been dismissed. By the time I got to the door, he was busy typing away.

Nothing.

That's what happens to the stepmother in *Cinderella*.

Nothing.

I just Googled the story because I remembered how in *Sleeping Beauty*, the fairy who caused all the trouble turns into a dragon and Prince Charming stabs her, and she dies this really horrible death. But there's nothing like that in *Cinderella*. In fact, you never find out what happens to Cinderella's stepmother or her stepsisters. As far as I can tell the three of them just spend their time hanging out, probably getting some new girl to bring them breakfast in bed and hand-wash their clothes. I guess you're supposed to think it's punishment enough that they have to live the rest of their lives knowing Cinderella's got this really hot husband and is living the perfect life, while they're just three ugly, mean ladies destined to grow old and die without ever getting a photo spread in *Palace Monthly*.

But what if Cinderella's life isn't so perfect? Like, what if Prince Charming throws up on Cinderella's boots after his team loses the big game? And what if the most popular girl in school implies that the only reason Cinderella's got the Prince in the first place is because she wasn't interested in him? And what if Cinderella gets grounded for an unspecified period of time? What if *that's* how the story ends? What if *that's* happily ever after?

Well, if you want my opinion, that sucks.

Chapter Eighteen

Mara was sitting at the kitchen table when I got up the next morning. Her back was to me, and walking around the table, I saw she was writing a thank-you note. That's basically her favorite activity, writing these really phony notes to her friends and acquaintances. *My dear Laura, How can I ever thank you for the lovely time we had yesterday evening? You are such a generous, delightful hostess. . . .*

"Hi," I said, trying not to sound as defeated as I felt. She wore a coordinated peach pantsuit, and her hair and makeup were flawless. It was as if she were planning to spend the day running for office.

"Hello, Lucy," she said, looking up at me.

"Um, listen," I said. I stood with my hands on the back of the chair opposite her, one foot resting on the ankle of the other, like a little kid.

"Yes?" she said. She kept her pen poised to write, making it clear I'd better talk fast.

"I just wanted to, you know, apologize for what I said the other night."

She pursed her lips. "Quite frankly, Lucy, I was shocked. No one has ever spoken to me like that before." I didn't know if she expected another apology, but if so, she wasn't getting it. I may not have wanted to be grounded for life, but even freedom is worth just so much ass-kissing.

I continued with the speech I'd planned out while brushing my teeth. "And your friend staying in my room—I mean, that's fine. I'll—it's fine for me to sleep in the den while she's here. I'm going to clean out my stuff—I mean, clean out—up—I'm going to clean up my room for her." My delivery had been much more polished when I was talking to my reflection in the mirror than it was now.

"Well," she said, "I'm certainly glad to see this change in your attitude." She nodded at me. "Your apology is accepted."

Was I supposed to thank her? I didn't say anything.

"Now," she continued, "since you're not going out with your friends tonight"—I loved how she phrased it as if the choice had been mine—"your father would like you to join us for dinner."

It didn't sound like the "invitation" was exactly optional, but I pretended to consider her offer for a second before saying, "Yeah, sure."

"Fine. Then we'll see you later," she said. I turned to go. "No jeans, tonight, please," she called after me.

Five minutes later I was back in bed, where I instantly fell asleep. The next thing I knew, there was a pounding on my door.

"What?" I yelled. I had that fuzzy, brainless feeling you get from sleeping way too long.

Somehow the Princesses heard my "What?" as "Come on in!" and they bounded down the stairs.

"You were *sleeping*?" said Princess One.

"No," I said. "Sometimes I just like to lie in the dark for hours with my eyes closed."

They both stared at me for a minute. "Are you joking?" Princess Two asked finally.

"Yes, I am joking," I said, yawning. "Now, what do you want?"

"Connor called," said Princess Two. "It's on the answering machine." She put her hands on her hips. "Is he, like, your boyfriend?"

"Yes," I said. I felt a little scared after I'd said it, as if I was jinxing myself.

"Julie Wexler told *us* that her sister told *her* that Connor's the most popular boy in school," said Princess One. Even in the pale light that filtered down from the kitchen, I could see the awe in her eyes. Julie Wexler had recently replaced Jennifer Johnson in the Princesses' best friend rotation; her pronouncements were repeated as if she, like an Old Testament prophet, spent most of her time communicating directly with God.

"I guess he's popular," I said, arching my back and yawning.

Princess Two eyed me briefly before turning toward the stairs. "Come on!" she called to her sister, "We have to get dressed."

Princess One walked along the bed, trailing her fingers across the comforter. She kept giving me sidelong glances, as if she wasn't comfortable staring directly at me.

"Come on!" her sister repeated impatiently, and she bolted for the stairs.

I rolled over, picked up the phone, and dialed Connor's number. "Hey," he said when he heard my voice. "I guess I got a little drunk last night."

"Just a little," I said.

Music pulsed in the background, and Connor rapped along with it for a second before saying, "I gotta make it up to you, Red. How can I make it up to you?"

Come over to my house and drive a stake through my stepmother's heart. "I don't know," I said.

"I bet it's gonna cost me." Somehow he managed to make the words sound a tiny bit like a threat, a tiny bit like a dare; either way, it was pretty sexy.

"I bet it is," I said. Did Connor like me enough to spend the rest of his life in jail for killing my stepmother? Maybe if I asked him while I was wearing that red dress. . . .

He lowered his voice. "Can I ask you something, or are you too mad?" I shivered. It felt like he was whispering in my ear.

"I don't know," I said, whispering, too. "That depends on what it is."

"Well, try this one on for size." He paused. "Think you might be willing to come to the prom with me?"

Aaaaahhhhh!

He'd asked me. He'd actually asked me. I shot up, miraculously managing to swallow a scream. Then I made myself sit down on the edge of the bed, cross my legs at the ankles, and speak calmly into the phone. "I think I might consider it," I said. But it was impossible to stay seated, and I jumped to my feet, hopping from one to the other.

"You kill me, Red," he said. "There's no one cooler than you are."

It was a good thing Connor couldn't see me, since I wasn't sure I looked all that cool leaping around in an oversized T-shirt and a pair of thick orange socks with holes in the heels, my hand pressed to my lips so no screams would escape.

I heard the click of someone picking up another extension. "Hello?" It was Mara.

Oh my god, now she was listening in on my calls to my father *and* my boyfriend.

"Yeah, hi, Mara. I'm on the phone."

"Lucy, you're awake. Why don't you come upstairs and say hello?"

"I—"

"Now," she said, and she hung up.

"I gotta go, Connor," I said.

"Call me later," he said. "Prom date."

I hung up the regular phone and grabbed my cell before Mara came down to confiscate it. Jessica picked up on the first ring. She didn't even say hello.

"Did Connor ask you?"

"Just now."

"Oh my god!" she screamed. "Dave asked me, like, five minutes ago, and Madison's on the phone with Matt *right now.*"

"We're going to the prom!" I wanted to shout it from the rooftops, but I kept my voice down. The last thing I needed was for my stepmother to know there was something in my life I was actually looking forward to. It would just make her that much more eager to take it away from me.

There was a knock on my door. "Lucy, Mom says you have to come upstairs now."

I lowered my voice to a whisper. "I gotta go."

"We're going to the prom," Jessica whispered.

"Why are you whispering?" I asked, starting to giggle.

"Why are *you* whispering?" she asked, giggling, too.

"I don't know," I said.

"Me either," she said. Then she started laughing for real, and so did I. "I'll call you later," she said.

I was laughing too hard to say anything else, so I just hung up the phone.

The dining room table was elaborately set for twelve, and soft classical music played in the living room, where Mara, my dad, and a woman I didn't recognize were sitting having drinks.

"Hey, honey," said my dad, spotting me. "Sure you got enough sleep?" I knew he was making a joke, and I forced myself to smile.

"I think so," I said. Then I walked over to the unknown woman and extended my hand. "I'm Lucy," I said.

"I'm Gail," she said. Except for her dyed blond hair, she could have been Mara's clone. They were both in dark silk skirts and pale fuzzy sweaters, and each held a glass of white wine in her hand.

I wondered if Gail knew she was going to be sleeping in my room, but it seemed impolite to ask. With Connor's invitation still ringing in my ear, I knew the last thing I could afford was for my dad to think I was being rude to Mara's friend. *Sorry, Connor, I know I said I could go to the prom with you, but I'm grounded.*

Forever.

I smiled broadly and turned to Mara. "Is there anything I can do to help?" I'd dressed in a blue silk dress I hadn't worn since I was about twelve. It was ugly as sin, but it wasn't jeans.

"Everything that needs to be taken care of for now is done," said Mara, "but I think it would be really nice if you and the girls would help serve drinks and dinner when the guests arrive."

Help serve drinks and dinner? What was I, the new maid? I kept the smile plastered on my face. *Prom. Prom. Prom. You're going to the prom.* "Sure," I said. "Glad to help." I started to feel silly just standing there in the middle of the room, so I excused myself. "I guess I'll drop this in the den," I said, picking up the bag I'd packed for my stint as an actual guest in my own house.

"Lucy, I was telling the girls I think it would be just charming if you all wore black and white tonight," Mara called after me. I turned back. "Don't you think that would look nice?"

"Oh, yeah," I said. "I think that would look really nice." Mara smiled at me like I'd just made all her dreams come true. I smiled back at her the same way. Actually, Mara had just made *one* of my dreams come true. I was going to see the Princesses forced to get up off their little Princess asses and help serve a meal.

Within two minutes of walking in the door, the Martins, the Allens, and the Clurmans had clearly gotten the idea that I was an employee as opposed to the daughter of their host, no doubt in part because A) I was dressed like a waitress at a cheesy catering hall, and B) Mara, rather than introduce me, said only, "Lucy, please take everyone's coats and put them on my bed." Despite Mara's saying that the Princesses and I would be serving *together*, I was the only one dressed like I'd be collecting a paycheck at the end of the evening. My stepsisters were sporting fashionable new black-and-white Petit Bateau shirts (Princess One had a white-on-black pattern, while Princess Two had gone with black-on-white) and tiny black miniskirts, ensembles no doubt purchased for this occasion. As far as I could tell, they weren't doing much besides "helping" my dad bartend, a task that involved little more than throwing the occasional lemon wedge or swizzle stick into the occasional glass. I, meanwhile, spent the first part of the evening running back and forth to the kitchen with plates of hot appetizers Mara had ordered from her favorite caterer. The platters were heavy, the kitchen was hot, and before long I'd developed a fairly gruesome headache. Mara, smiling and chatting with her guests, barely acknowledged me as I walked around the room offering cheese puffs.

"You're doing a great job," said my dad when he came into the kitchen to get more ice. I was standing by the stove watching to make sure the spinach in phyllo dough didn't burn. "This is what I like to see." He came over and gave my shoulder a squeeze. "This is the girl I always knew you could be."

He always knew I could be a maid?

I opened my mouth to tell him what *I'd* always known *he* could be, but then I got a picture of myself lying prone on my bed, carving lines in my Formica headboard to mark the months of my imprisonment, while Connor slipped a corsage onto his new girlfriend's wrist and escorted her to their waiting limo.

"I'm glad, Dad," I said, smiling weakly. "I'm really glad." I watched him leave the kitchen and turned back to the oven.

I'll never know if the Martins, the Allens, or the Clurmans ever figured out who I was, or if they just decided my dad and Mara were incredibly enlightened employers who allowed the help to sit down and eat with them and their guests whenever she wasn't serving a new course. Since each platter that had to be carried in from the kitchen was too heavy for the Princesses to manage, the job was mine. It wasn't until dessert, when they exerted themselves so far as to circulate a tiny plate of petits fours, that either of them did any serving at all; as they walked around the table, the guests oohed and aahed over how helpful and gracious they were. I stood watching them help themselves to as many pastries as they "served," brushing my now-matted hair out of my eyes and seething with rage. By the time I carried the coats down from my dad and Mara's room and distributed them among the guests, I wasn't even surprised that Mr. Martin complimented me for doing such a great job and asked if I was available to help him and his wife with a party they were having the following weekend. I couldn't tell if he was joking or not, so I just said I was grounded and handed him his coat.

"Lucy, you did a beautiful job tonight," said my dad. He'd shut the door on the last of the guests and put his arm around Mara. "You *and* the girls, I should say."

"Yes, thank you, Lucy," said Mara. "Good night."

"Good night," I said.

As Mara climbed the stairs, my dad yawned. "I guess I'll turn in, too," he said. "And you must be exhausted."

I didn't need a mirror to know that my hair was plastered to my forehead and my white shirt was streaked with sweat. My feet ached. I looked up and saw Mara's skirt magically unwrinkled, her hair shining in the overhead light.

"Yeah," I said, wondering where my fairy god-mother had spent the night. "I'm a little tired."

"Well, good night, honey."

"Good night, dad," I said. He turned to go up the stairs, then turned back again. "Tonight it really felt like we were a family," he said, smiling at me.

Did that mean I wasn't grounded anymore?

"Um, Dad?"

"Yeah, Goose?"

Maybe this wasn't the best time to ask. "See you in the morning."

He reached over and patted me on the head before turning and following Mara up the stairs. I took off my apron and was about to open the door to the basement when I remembered I was sleeping in the guest room for the week.

Did my dad seriously think that tonight we were a family?

If so, get me to an orphanage.

Chapter Nineteen

Monday at lunch Jessica and Madison wanted me to hang out in the cafeteria so we could discuss the newly announced prom theme (Now and Forever), but I begged off. If I didn't get started on my self-portrait, I was going to fail the only class I was taking that I didn't hate.

When I got to the studio, Ms. Daniels was sitting at her desk going through Gardner's *Art Through the Ages* with a pile of Post-its. She gave me a little wave.

"Feeling artistic?" she asked.

"Panicked," I corrected, going over to her desk. "This never happened to me before. I just can't figure out how to start."

"Well, what if you start by thinking about a painting that means a lot to you?"

"You mean rip something off?"

Ms. Daniels laughed. "I mean consider using it as a

commentary on who you are." She took the heavy textbook in both hands and passed it over the desk to me, grunting with the effort. "Here. I've got to get to a meeting. Why don't you look for yourself."

Two-thirds of the way through the book, I still couldn't see the point of Ms. Daniels's exercise. Did she really expect ten million pictures of Renaissance churches to inspire one twenty-first-century portrait?

"Hey."

I looked up to see Sam standing by the end of the couch. I hadn't even heard him come in. "Hey, yourself," I said.

"Thanks again for coming Friday night." He took off his glasses and rubbed one of the lenses with his shirt-tail. "It was great having you there." He put his glasses back on and gave me a really nice smile.

"It was great being there," I said. "Thanks for inviting me." With everything that had happened since I'd left Sam in the city, I'd almost forgotten how cool it had been to be at the gallery. I was actually really glad to see him.

"Did you make it back in time for the 'big game'?" he asked, putting quotation marks around the last two words.

"Ha, ha. As a matter of fact, I did."

"What a Renaissance woman you are," he said. "Art. Sports." He looked down at the book in my lap. "And you're even looking at *pictures* of the

Renaissance." He shook his head in mock amazement. "Incredible."

"You're hilarious."

"It's a gift." He looked around the room. "Seen Ms. Daniels?"

"She's got a meeting."

He whistled softly to himself. "No worries," he said, slinging his backpack over his shoulder. "Catch you later."

"Later," I said.

Sam's interruption seemed as good an excuse as any to give up on my self-imposed exile and go find Jessica and Madison in the cafeteria. But then I flipped to the end of the book, and suddenly I was staring at a reproduction of *The Dancers*. It was a little weird to come upon a painting I felt so possessive of there in *Art Through the Ages* for everybody to see. I looked at Matisse's strange, fluid figures and touched my finger to the shiny page. Maybe I could—

"Hel-*lo*!"

"Okay, we can't live without you." It was Madison and Jessica.

"Hey, check this out." I turned the book toward them.

"Cool," said Madison, but she didn't really look at the painting.

"We have the sickest gossip for you," said Jessica.

"Kathryn and her boyfriend broke up," said Madison.

"No way," I said.

"Way!" said Madison. "She wanted to go to the prom with him, and he said he didn't want to party with a bunch of high-school kids. He's, like, thirty years old or something."

"He's twenty," Jessica corrected her.

"Whatev," said Madison. "Isn't that crazy?"

"Totally," I said, closing the book. I'd deal with my self-portrait later. I stood up and grabbed Connor's jacket, dropping *Art Through the Ages* on Ms. Daniels's desk as I walked past.

"I wonder if she'll ask a junior, like Jane Brown did," said Jessica, holding the door for me.

Sam accepting an invitation to the prom seemed so mainstream of him. I figured he must really like Jane.

"Just as long as she doesn't ask a sophomore," said Madison. "We three are the only sophomores going."

"Speaking of which," said Jessica, "do you want to look at dresses after school?"

I shook my head. "Can't," I said. "I'm meeting Connor."

At three-ten, when I got to the exit by the senior parking lot, Connor was already there.

And he was talking to Kathryn Ford.

Kathryn's tiny, perfect shoulders were up against a locker, while the rest of her body formed a triangle with the wall and the floor. Connor stood over her, looking into her Barbie-blue eyes and nodding emphatically. She reached up and brushed something out of his hair.

"Hey, Lucy!" Somehow sensing my presence, Kathryn swiveled her head in my direction but left the rest of her body facing Connor, like a praying mantis.

Or a cobra.

I walked over to where they were standing.

"How's it goin', Red?"

"Um, okay." Standing so close to Kathryn, I suddenly felt enormous, like one of those giants that entire towns must unite to defeat. "Thanks again for the ride Friday," I said to her.

"Oh, sure," she said. "Tonight, though, it's me passed out in the passenger seat." She hip checked Connor. "You're driving, right?"

"No way, José," he said. "Senior City Night? I'm crawling."

"Well, I gotta cruise," said Kathryn. "See you kids later." She peeled herself off the wall and brushed her hair forward over her right shoulder. It positively gleamed. Gleamed. As if she'd stepped out of a Pantene ad. "Bye, bro." Kathryn stood on her tiptoes and wrapped not just her arms but her entire body around Connor. While they were still embracing, she turned to me. "Doesn't he just give the best hugs?"

Kathryn, perhaps you'd care to take a bite of this shiny, red apple I have in my hand. I made it specially for you.

"Oh, yeah," I said, snapping out of my reverie. "Totally."

Finally they let go of each other, and Kathryn started down the hall.

"Come on," Connor said to me, shouldering the door open. "Let's go get something to eat." As we crossed the senior parking lot, it was hard to erase from my mind the memory of Kathryn pressing her body up against Connor's. What if tonight in the city he suddenly realized he was tired of me, that I wasn't fun enough or cool enough or . . . Kathryn enough? But just as I was picturing the two of them riding off into the sunset together, Connor's SUV towering protectively over Kathryn's mini, Connor picked me up and threw me over his shoulder.

"Who's my girl?" he asked.

"Connor, put me down!" I screamed.

"Say it," he said. "Who's my girl?" He mock slapped me on the butt.

"Connor," I repeated, laughing, "put me down."

"Not until you say it."

"I am!" I yelled. "I am. Now put me down."

"That's more like it," he said, and when he put me down and wrapped his arms around me, the perfect kiss he planted with his perfect lips perfectly deleted the image I'd just had of my perfectly princeless future.

* * *

At dinner my stepmother not only directly addressed me, she actually made my day.

"Lucy, your father and I discussed it, and we want to thank you for being such a big help on Saturday night. We really appreciate it. You should feel free to make whatever plans you want for Friday night."

I didn't even wait for my dad to call, just hightailed it downstairs as soon as dinner was over and dialed Connor's cell.

"Yo, what's up? It's Connor. You know what to do."

"Hey, it's me," I said. "I have good news. Call me later." After I left the message, I realized Connor hadn't known I was grounded—I'd told him I needed to be home right after our afternoon deli-run, but I hadn't told him why. So maybe my being un-grounded wouldn't qualify as good news to him.

Still, it was good news to me.

The day after Senior City Night was Senior Cut Day. I didn't know if it was Connor's being absent, but everything seemed a little unreal, like I was walking around in a watercolor instead of a three-dimensional world. I couldn't focus at all. In math, Jessica took advantage of Mr. Palmer's chewing out John Marcus for answering his cell during class to ask if Connor had told me the details of how last night he, Matt, and Dave all puked on the street outside some club.

I shook my head.

"Sometimes those guys totally piss me off," she whispered. "Matt told Madison they were doing shots of tequila all night." She made a face. "Whatever. Hey, do you want to go look at prom dresses after school?"

"Miss Johnson, Miss Norton, are you *quite* ready for tomorrow's *quiz*?" Mr. Palmer was glaring at Jessica from the front of the room.

"Sorry, Mr. Palmer," said Jessica.

"Yeah, sorry," I said. When he went back to writing on the board, Jessica rolled her eyes at me. I nodded, but I couldn't quite stave off the flicker of anxiety in the pit of my stomach. Dave had called Jessica. Matt had called Madison.

Why hadn't Connor called me?

After class, Madison met Jessica and me in the hallway.

"Okay, are we prom dress–shopping it later?" Jessica asked as we walked to the cafeteria.

"Let's wait until spring break," said Madison. "My mom's totally on my case about this warning notice I got in math." She took a swig of water and pushed open the door of the cafeteria with her hip. "Matt said he threw up six times already," she said. "How totally gross is that?"

"Totally," Jessica agreed. "Dave said he'd been puking all morning."

I didn't say anything, very self-conscious about the fact that I had no idea how many times Connor had puked in the past twenty-four hours. It *was* what they wanted to hear, right? *Well, Matt may have thrown up six times and Dave may have been throwing up all morning, but since he is the most popular boy in school, Connor, naturally, has thrown up more than both of them put together. I know this because I am his girlfriend and, as such, am responsible for disseminating information about His Majesty's gastrointestinal functions.*

They sat down at an empty table. "I just need to get a sandwich," I said, not sitting.

Both Madison and Jessica gave me a look. "What?" I asked.

"You okay?" asked Madison.

I shrugged. "Yeah, sure."

Jessica reached for my hand. "Looocy," she said, sounding just like Ricky Ricardo. "You got some 'splainin' to do."

I pulled out a chair, sat down, and closed my eyes, too embarrassed by what I was about to say to look at them. "Connor hasn't called me all day."

Jessica started laughing, and so did Madison. But when I didn't join them, they stopped. I opened my eyes. "You're not seriously worried about that?" asked Jessica.

"It's been, like, twenty-four hours," I said.

Jessica put her arm around me. "Honey, he is *so* into you."

"You think?" I asked, feeling better already.

"Totally," said Madison. "He's probably way too busy praying to the porcelain god to remember to call."

"Maybe you're right," I said.

"No maybe about it," she said.

As I crossed the cafeteria to buy my sandwich, I felt about a million times happier than I had five minutes ago, though I had to admit my good mood wasn't exactly born of altruism. I mean, Jessica had just convinced me that my boyfriend was physically unable to lift a telephone. Shouldn't I have been overwhelmed with sympathy and concern?

But instead of being sad for him, I felt glad for me. Because everyone knows it's better to have a boyfriend who feels too sick to call than one who just doesn't feel like calling at all.

Chapter Twenty

After school I went to the studio. The idea I'd gotten looking at *The Dancers* yesterday had stayed with me, and the longer I worked on my sketch, the stronger my feeling grew that this idea might go the distance. I barely took my eyes off the page all afternoon, and the one time I did, I made eye contact with Ms. Daniels, who'd looked up at that exact second.

"You look pretty intent there," she said, gesturing to my sketch pad. "I've been taking that as a good sign."

"Here's hoping," I said.

"Want to show me what you've got?"

I looked down at what I'd been drawing. "Yeah, sure," I said, not feeling sure at all. I unfolded my legs and went over to her desk, where she looked up at me expectantly.

I pressed my notebook to my chest. "I'm afraid you're going to hate it," I said.

"Do *you* hate it?" she asked.

"No."

"Do you *like* it?"

I nodded.

"Well, why would I hate it if you like it?"

"Because you hated all the other ones."

She laughed. "First of all, I didn't hate them. I said I didn't think they were going to yield a self-portrait that was very interesting. And second of all, if you'd defended any one of them for even a second, I would have let you convince me."

I couldn't believe what she was saying. "Seriously?"

"Seriously. You just never seemed particularly excited about any of the drawings you showed me."

"I guess," I said, and even though I sounded hesitant, I knew what she'd said was true. All the other ideas I'd considered had been born of desperation, not inspiration.

"Now," she said, holding out her hand. "Let's see what you've got for me."

Silently, I handed over my sketch. Ms. Daniels looked it up and down, not saying anything. Then she took my pencil from me.

Uh-oh, here it comes.

"See how there are three figures here and none here? You could move this one up just a little, and it might be more balanced. Then you'd have less empty space here," she pointed at the left side of the page, which was almost entirely blank, "and more here."

Did this mean . . .

"Wait, are you saying I can . . . that it's, you know, okay?"

She looked up at me. "Do *you* think it's okay?"

I looked at the figures I'd drawn, a line of Lucys holding hands, each just a little bit different from the others and looking off in a slightly different direction. The way they were simultaneously connected and yet isolated, each looking at something different, but looking at it the same way, expressed something about who I am that I didn't think I'd be able to put into words. I hoped Ms. Daniels wouldn't ask me to explain it.

"I *really* like it," I said.

"I thought so," she said. "And I, for one, think it's worthy of you. So why don't you start painting tomorrow?"

"Seriously?"

Ms. Daniels smiled. "Seriously."

Right then Sam came over to stand on the far side of the desk.

"Sorry, am I interrupting something?" he asked.

"We're done," I said, flipping my sketchbook closed. Even as I said the words, I didn't quite believe them.

"Well then, if it's okay with you," he said to

Ms. Daniels, "I'll take that painting home now."

Ms. Daniels made a sad face. "I guess I can't keep it forever." She looked over at the wall, and I realized they were talking about the painting of the tree that I liked so much. "But—and I'm not just saying this to hold on to it for one more day—I don't think you can carry it by yourself, and I've got a meeting in about . . ." She looked at the clock. ". . . Three minutes. So if you want to hang out until five-thirty I can do it. Or we could wait until tomorrow."

"Can I help?"

They both turned to look at me.

"Are you sure you don't mind?" asked Ms. Daniels. "It's not heavy, it's just cumbersome."

"Really, you don't have to," said Sam. "I can bring it home another time."

"No," I said. "I'd like to." It was the least I could do considering how he'd invited me to my first and only New York gallery opening. Besides—it would be fun to hang out with Sam. "Just tell me what to do."

I couldn't see how the enormous painting we were carrying had a snowball's chance in hell of fitting into the backseat of Sam's car—a gorgeous, yellow VW bug that dated back to the days of Jimi Hendrix and Janis Joplin—without getting completely scratched up. Luckily I didn't voice my doubts, since with just a little pulling and pushing, the canvas slid easily into the minuscule space; there was even room for us to sit in the front with our seats more or less upright.

"That was incredible," I said, shaking my head with awe as we pulled out of the parking lot. "I won't lie to you—when I first saw the proportions of the objects in question, I had some concerns."

"Oh, ye of little faith," said Sam. He stopped the car and turned to me. "Wait. Where am I taking you?"

"Home, I guess." I gave him my address.

"I'm sure I'll be able to recognize it," he said, driving on. "It's the one with the turret room accessible only by ponytail, right?"

"Well, yes and no. There *is* a secret tunnel that runs under the moat to the basement where I'm locked up at night, but it's guarded by a fairly aggressive dragon."

"Of course," said Sam. "I would have been disappointed with anything less." Without taking his eyes of the road, Sam fished around the pocket of his car door for a CD, found it, and popped it in. *Subterranean Homesick Blues* filled the car as Sam reached across me and opened the glove compartment. I thought he was looking for a different CD, but he took out a box of Raisinets. "Chocolate?" he asked, holding the box between his knees as he opened it one-handed.

"Sure," I said, and he shook some into my hand.

"So, how's it going? I see your stepmother has yet to hire a local woodsman to take you into the forest and kill you."

"Well, she tried," I said, throwing a few Raisinets into my mouth. "But it's really hard to get good help nowadays. You'd be amazed how much trouble she's having just *finding* a local woodsman."

"These things take time," acknowledged Sam. We drove along in silence until finally I couldn't keep quiet about what was on my mind for one more second.

"Guess what," I said, when we stopped for a red light. I was almost giggling with excitement.

"What?" asked Sam. He looked over at me expectantly.

Sam's look made me feel a little silly. I mean, it wasn't like my news was all that thrilling. Still, it felt thrilling to *me*. "I finally got an idea for my self-portrait."

"Hey, that's great," said Sam, smiling. A car behind us honked, and Sam put the car in gear. "Can I ask what it is, or are you not ready to say yet?"

I wrinkled my face and shook my head. "I don't mean to be rude, but . . ."

"Wait, you're worried that I'll judge your poor etiquette?" asked Sam, laughing. "Didn't you once nominate me for the Rudest-Person-Alive Award?"

I turned toward him. "Oh, yeah, what ever happened with that?" I asked.

He made the left onto my block. "They gave it to some guy in Manhattan who clips his nails on the subway."

"Too bad," I said. "Are you upset?"

Sam shrugged. "Win some, lose some." I pointed out my house, and Sam pulled up in front of it and killed the engine. "Do you mind if I ask what your inspiration was?"

"Gardner's *Art Through the Ages.* I'm a shameless thief," I admitted.

"Well, like Picasso said, 'Good artists borrow. Great artists steal.' And as you know, I myself have stolen more than my fair share of ideas. Which is not to say I'm a great artist," he added quickly.

"I don't know," I said. "You're pretty great." I watched a blush creep up his cheeks as he tapped out a drum solo on the steering wheel in an attempt to ignore what I'd just said. "God, you're so easy to embarrass," I said. "Look at you, turning all red."

"Come on," he said. I watched him fight the smile teasing the corner of his mouth.

"This is so much fun," I said. "It could be a new parlor game. Make Sam Blush."

"Ha ha," he said.

"What a brilliant artist you are, Sam," I said loudly. "What natural talent. What technique."

Sam was smiling, but he was also beet red. "Are you going to stop?"

"And your brushwork." I kissed the tips of my fingers. "It's nothing short of genius."

He turned on the engine. "Well, bye, Lucy. Thanks for all your help."

"Not to mention your extraordinary use of color."

"Really, thanks for everything." He cranked up the volume on Dylan's wail.

"Seriously, Sam, you should rent yourself out for parties. You're more reliable than Old Faithful."

Sam cupped his hand around his ear. "What's that, Lucy?" he shouted. "You say you have to go?"

"Actually, I do have to go," I shouted back. Teasing Sam was pretty great, but I'd told Madison I'd check out a dress she'd e-mailed me a picture of. It was already later than I'd expected to get home. If I didn't call soon, she could go into prom dress-related conversation withdrawal.

"Thanks for the ride," I said, as I opened the door.

Sam held his hands out and then pointed from the stereo to his ear, shaking his head. "Sorry, Lucy, can't hear a word you're saying," he shouted. "Thanks again."

Laughing, I shut the door and watched Sam pull away from the curb just as my cell phone rang. I grabbed it. "I'm walking into the house as we speak," I said. "I'll look at it and call you right back."

"Five minutes," she said.

"Five minutes," I promised. I'd been planning on grabbing a snack, but now I figured I'd better go online first. When you say you'll call someone in five minutes, you can't call them in twenty.

Being royalty is no excuse for being rude.

Chapter Twenty-one

When Connor finally got around to calling, it was easy to tell that my paranoid fantasies of him riding off into the sunset with Kathryn Ford were a little misplaced.

"Hey, Red," he said. He sounded really bad. "Sorry I haven't called. I've been kinda sick."

"Yeah, you don't sound so good."

"I don't feel so good. Me and Matt and Dave started throwing back shots of tequila." There was a pause, and I heard Connor swallow. "I can't even talk about it." His voice was thin, as if it took effort to speak.

I felt terrible for him. "Are you okay?" I'd never been hung over, but I once spent twenty-four hours throwing up from a bad clam.

"I'll live. But what's your good news?"

For a second I couldn't remember, then it came back

to me. "Oh, I was potentially grounded forever, but now I'm not."

"That's awesome, Red."

There was a knock at my door. "Lucy," called Princess Two, "dinner."

"Connor, can I call you back? My stepmother goes insane if I'm not upstairs for dinner at seven on the dot."

Connor groaned. "Don't say dinner. Please."

Like the painting of a masterpiece, the search for the perfect prom dress is not a matter to be undertaken lightly. One must have the single-mindedness of purpose, the courage, the blind devotion to the task at hand of a true believer. One must have strength. One must have vision.

One must have one's father's credit card.

To obtain said father's credit card, I spent the first Saturday of spring break being ordered around by Mara, who wanted to see what the living room would look like if the couch was where the love seat was and the love seat was in the den. As I moved glass figurines, end tables, and a hideous grandfather clock around the house, I knew Jessica and Madison were at Miracle Mile, wrapping themselves in silk and satin, being waited on hand and foot by obsequious salesladies catering to their every whim. But a girl's gotta do what a girl's gotta do, and Monday, when I walked into Roses Are Red with my dad's Visa in the back pocket of my jeans, I knew my blood, sweat, and tears had paid off.

"This one is nice," said Madison, extracting a pale pink dress from where it was wedged between two other pink ones. We were waiting for the saleslady to come back with the dress Madison had put on hold Saturday. "I tried it on but it made me look all washed out."

I looked at the dress. "I don't know, Madison," I said. "Pink?"

She put the dress back and came over to me. "You know what you have to do?" She stared intensely into my eyes. "You have to *picture* yourself on prom night, okay?"

The saleslady came out from the back. "I'm sorry, dear, I just don't think we have the dress you're describing."

From across the store, Jessica rolled her eyes at me and spun her finger next to her temple.

"Are you kidding?" asked Madison, turning to the woman. "I was just here Saturday."

The saleslady smiled vaguely. "Are you *sure* you have the right store? Because there are so many—"

"Oh my god," said Madison, "can I just come back there and look?" Before the woman had a chance to answer, Madison had pushed past her, through the curtains and into the nether regions of the store. I gave the saleslady a little shrug, and she smiled at me, fluttering her hands in the air nervously.

"It's right *here*," said Madison, emerging from the back with a garment bag. "It's here."

"Oh, yes!" said the saleslady. She clapped her hands together. "*Now* I remember. You're having it taken in."

"She's deciding whether to buy it," corrected Jessica.

"Of course," said the woman, moving toward Madison and taking the dress from her. "Just follow me." She disappeared behind the curtains.

Madison came back to where I was standing. "Think about what I said. You have to *picture* it."

"Okay," I said. "I will."

She gave a little hop of excitement. "Just wait until you see my dress!" she squealed, turning toward the dressing area. "It's a-*mazing*." Halfway to the curtain, she stopped and turned back to us. "But you have to swear you'll say if you hate it, okay? Be brutally honest." I placed my hand over my heart.

"Scout's honor," I said.

While Madison was in the back, Jessica and I plunged into the racks of dresses. Most were really tacky—tulle, sequins, tulle and sequins, more tulle. The store's selection and Madison's reverence for pink was starting to make me a little nervous about the dress she'd chosen. What if she emerged from the dressing room looking like a Hostess cupcake? Just as I was about to ask Jessica to define what Madison meant by "brutally honest," Madison stepped out from between the curtains.

She looked like a movie star.

"Oh my god, Madison! It's . . . you're . . . wow." The dress was claret silk, strapless, with a sweetheart top and a tight bodice that ended in a full skirt. There was not so much as a speck of tulle. The saleslady hurried over and expertly pinned up Madison's hair.

"Madison, you look amazing," said Jessica. "It's definitely my favorite."

Madison spun around "Don't I look thin?"

"Emaciated," I said.

"Basically, you're like the thinnest person on the planet," added Jessica.

"So should I get it?" she asked.

"Are you kidding?" I said. "Buy it immediately."

She did a little shimmy of excitement. "Okay, I'm going to," she said, checking herself out one more time in the mirror and smiling at what she saw. Then she turned around and faced me. "Jessica's got two dresses on hold at Kewpid," she said. "So you're next."

Madison made me sit down on a tiny love seat in the dressing area, close my eyes, and picture the prom. She walked me through the whole night, starting with cocktails at her house, ending with my romantic slow dance with Connor as we were crowned prom king and queen.

"Now," she said finally, "quick: what are you wearing?"

I opened my eyes and looked at her. "I'm sorry, Madison," I said.

"Nothing?" I could tell she was really disappointed,

so I closed my eyes for another minute. Then I opened them again and shook my head.

"Sorry."

She sat down next to me, letting out a sigh. "Wow, I really thought it would work."

I patted her knee. "It's not your fault. I'm just not a very spiritual person." I wanted to sound reassuring, but suddenly I was fighting back panic. What if my inability to picture myself on prom night was a sign? What if I spent every free minute between now and prom searching for a dress, but I never found the right one? How can you be prom queen in jeans and a T-shirt?

Just then, Jessica poked her head through the curtains. "You guys aren't still trying that visualization crap are you?"

"It's not crap," said Madison. "The Dalai Lama says—"

"When His Holiness gets a *Vogue* column, Lucy will take his fashion advice," said Jessica, stepping through the curtains. In her arms was a long, dark blue dress. "Until then she needs more worldly assistance." Standing in front of me, she tossed the bottom part of the dress onto my lap, stepping back so the whole thing unfolded between us.

"I don't know, Jessica," I said. Jessica's selection wasn't doing much to alleviate my growing sense of panic. Even though I know a dress looks different on a person than on a hanger, I was pretty sure I didn't need to see this particular dress on my particular person to know it was not the dress for me. The bodice, which seemed to be made out of a heavy silk, was probably okay, but the skirt looked like it had the potential to be extremely tacky. "Chiffon?"

"It's the new velvet," said Jessica. "Trust me."

I didn't want to be rude, but chiffon reminds me a whole lot of tulle. Were there sequins on it? I took the hanger from Jessica while working on the wording of a polite refusal. Remembering how passionately Jessica and Madison had fought for me to buy the red dress, I realized I'd have to have more in my arsenal than, *It's not quite my style.* How about, *I hate it because I look like a tacky whore?*

But as I dropped the dress over my head and felt the rich fabric slide smoothly down my body, I wondered just how tacky such a delicious-feeling dress could be. And when I checked myself out in the mirror, I didn't have to wonder. The answer was clear—not tacky at all.

The bodice was tight silk, straight across in front, low-cut in the back, and strapless like Madison's. I'd expected the skirt to be poufy, just right for an extra in *Gone with the Wind*, but it hung almost straight down to the middle of my calves. It wasn't see-through, but you could just make out the shape of my legs through the filmy, delicate fabric. My skin seemed to glow against the dark blue silk. I couldn't believe it. I looked . . . beautiful.

When I stepped out of the dressing room and saw the expression on Jessica and Madison's faces, I knew I'd been right about how I looked. I twirled around, just like Madison had.

"Lucy, you look amazing," said Madison. "I can't believe you found the perfect dress on the first try!"

"*Who* found the perfect dress?" corrected Jessica.

"Ladies, I'm going to the ball," I said.

I started to laugh, and so did Jessica and Madison. "You mean the *prom*," said Madison through her laughter.

I shook my head, still laughing, and didn't bother to correct her.

Chapter Twenty-two

It wasn't until the end of the week that Jessica found a dress she liked, so we wound up spending every second of spring break shopping. I'd kind of planned on using the vacation to do some sketches for the landscape I was supposedly ready to start (now that the class, with the single exception of me, had finished self-portraits, we'd moved on to landscapes). But how can you tell your friend she's on her own after she helped you find the world's perfect prom dress?

You can't.

Which is why, as soon as we were back at school, I not only spent every one of my free periods in the studio frantically sketching my landscape *and* working on my self-portrait but also decided if I just cut math one little time—

"Done," I said.

Sam, the only other person in the room, was sketching on the couch.

"Did you say something?" he asked.

I didn't turn around, too amazed by what had just happened to move. "I'm done," I repeated, my voice flat. For the past two months, I'd been dreaming of this moment, fantasizing what it would feel like to put the whole horrible, impossible, frustrating project behind me. I'd thought as soon as I completed the final brushstroke I'd dance down the halls of Glen Lake, tipping my top hat at passers by. *I'm done! I'm done!* But now that I'd actually finished, I didn't feel like celebrating at all. I just felt . . . nothing.

I could hear Sam applauding. "Can I see it?"

"Um . . . Yeah, sure." The irony of his asking if he could see it was that even though I was standing less than a foot away from my easel, I couldn't see what I'd painted. Shapes and colors swirled around on the canvas in front of me, refusing to form themselves into a coherent image. Was this my self-portrait, this series of meaningless blobs?

Sam came over beside me and studied the painting. He stared at it for a long time, not saying anything, and I wondered what lies he'd use to assure me that my abstract mess wasn't an abstract mess. "Lucy," he said finally, "it's incredible."

I wanted to ask him what he meant, how he could say that, what he thought he was looking at, but I was afraid he'd think I was fishing for compliments. *What do you mean, what do I mean? I just told you it's incredible.*

And then, as if he could read my mind, Sam started to talk. "It's great how all the Lucy figures are holding hands even though they're looking off in different directions." I looked from one Lucy to the next as he talked, following his voice, watching his finger float above the canvas.

"And that one"—he pointed at the smallest Lucy—"the way it's barely holding on to the one next to it." He nodded. "You can feel her trying to catch up. It's brilliant."

"Actually, that one's a mistake." I tried to laugh. "See, I started in the wrong place, so I couldn't get the hand right."

Without taking his eyes off the canvas, Sam shrugged. "So?" He bumped his shoulder into mine. "It makes the painting, Lucy. Believe me."

He stayed there, leaning against me for another minute before going back to the couch. Even after he walked away and left me staring at my canvas, I could still feel the soft cotton of his T-shirt against my bare skin. And then, all at once, as if Sam had been speaking not words but brushstrokes, I saw my painting, saw it just the way he had. And as the shifting maze of shape and color solidified into forms, I realized that last Lucy *didn't* look like a mistake. It *did* make the painting better. Because of her, because she looked like she was running to catch up, the whole line of Lucys seemed to be moving. Sam was right. It really was a brilliant mistake.

I was so focused on my painting, I'd almost forgotten about Sam still being in the room with me, when suddenly he said, "You know, I've been meaning to—"

Just then the door flew open. It was Madison and Jessica, and when they saw me, they high-fived.

"Told you she'd be here," said Jessica.

"Hey, guys," I said. I was glad they'd shown up. Thanks to Sam I couldn't wait to show off my painting. It was just how I'd imagined finishing it would feel.

"Hey, Sam," said Jessica.

"Hey, Jessica," said Sam. He and Madison nodded at each other.

"Okay," Madison said to me from the doorway, "you can cut math, but you can't cut lunch."

"Yeah," said Jessica, as her cell started ringing, "no starving artists allowed at prom." She dug around in her bag for her phone.

"Hello? Hang on." She turned to Madison. "My mom wants to know if your mom wants her to do anything for the cocktail party at your house. Should she call her?"

"I thought they talked already," said Madison.

I turned back to Sam on the couch. "What were you going to say?"

"I've been meaning to . . ." he stopped and shook his head. "I've been meaning to get going for the past half hour." He stood up. "But I really like your painting." He grabbed his bag off the floor.

"No, Mom, I said *fifty*," said Jessica. "Not *fifteen*."

"Thanks," I said to Sam's back. "Your critique almost makes me feel like an artist."

As he pushed open the door of the studio, Sam turned around. "You *are* an artist," he said. Then he disappeared into the hall.

Jessica hung up the phone. "Okay, my mother is officially retarded." She turned to Madison. "I hope your mother is prepared to plan this cocktail party with an actual retarded person."

"Please," said Madison, "my mom's so retarded she makes your mom look like Einstein."

Jessica went over to where my bag and Connor's jacket were lying on the floor and picked them up. "Lunch, madam?"

"Sure," I said, reluctantly stepping away from my painting. "I could eat."

"Good," said Jessica. "Because we have an official prom update for you."

"What?"

"Which homecoming queen has reunited with her million-year-old boyfriend and is therefore bagging the Glen Lake prom?"

"No way!" I said.

Madison nodded. "Totally," she said.

As Jessica came over to where I was standing she glanced at my easel. "Wow, I like your painting." She pointed at the biggest of the Lucy figures. "Is that you?" When I nodded, she smiled. "It totally looks like you."

Madison came over to see what we were looking at. "Ohmygod! Did you paint this?" asked Madison, looking from me to the painting. "It's amazing."

"Yeah," I said. "It's the self-portrait I was telling you about."

"Oh!" Madison exclaimed. "That's you!" she pointed at one of the smallest of the Lucy figures.

"Wait," said Jessica. "I thought that one was you."

Madison looked where Jessica was pointing. "Hey," she said. "That *is* you."

Jessica turned to me. "How come there are so many of you?"

"It's kind of how—"

"Is it like clones?" asked Madison.

"Well, not exactly. It's more—" Why had this seemed so much easier when I was talking to Sam?

"It's really cool," said Jessica. "You're mondo talented. Now—" She took me by the arm and steered me away from the easel. "We must discuss Kathryn's skanky boyfriend and post-prom Hamptons clothing options."

"As in, what do we need to shop for," Madison explained, following us.

"So, come along, Prom Queen," said Jessica, as she pulled open the studio door. "Your loyal court attends you."

As we walked along the hall, I linked my arms through theirs. Maybe Jessica and Madison didn't get all the nuances of my painting that Sam did. But I was still glad they were my friends.

Chapter Twenty-three

A few hours later, as I stood in front of the open freezer debating the nutritional benefits of chicken nuggets versus sorbet as an after-school snack, my cell rang. It was my dad.

"Hey," I said. I looked at the wall clock. "It's Friday. Aren't you supposed to be on a plane right now?"

"Hi, Goose. I'm still in San Francisco," he said. "We're fogged in."

"Big surprise," I said. I opened the sorbet. There was about half a spoonful left in the container. I put it back.

"Is Mara there?" he asked.

"Nope." I took the chicken nuggets out of the freezer.

"Well, I'm having trouble getting her on her cell: could you just leave her a message that I'm stuck here and I'm hoping to get a flight at least as far as Chicago tonight?"

I tossed the nuggets on a plate and put it in the microwave. "Check, chief."

"How about you, Goose, big plans with your big man?"

"Big plans, big man," I said. Really we were just going to Piazzolla's and a movie. But it was big enough.

"Sounds like fun," said my dad. "Hey, did you get my e-mail about the Andy Goldsworthy?" Andy Goldsworthy is an artist my dad and I both love, and he had a sculpture show opening on the roof of the Met this weekend.

"Um . . ." Was I really up for a repeat performance of *Dad and Mara Ignore Lucy at the Museum*? Luckily the kitchen phone started ringing before I could answer him. I looked to see who was calling.

"It's Mara," I said.

"Oh, great," he said. "Tell her my plan, okay? And tell her I'll keep trying her on her cell."

"Okay," I said. "Love you."

"Love you, too, honey. And tell Mara I love her."

That was so not part of the message I'd be delivering. I tossed the nugget box back in the freezer and grabbed the phone.

"Hi, Lucy, it's Mara. Is your father home yet?" I could tell she was calling from her car. "My battery's all messed up on my cell. I think he's been trying to reach me."

The microwave beeped. "He's in California."

"What?" From her high-pitched wail, you'd have thought I'd said, *He's with his divorce lawyer.*

If only.

"He's still in California." I took the plate of nuggets out. "They're fogged in. He said he tried to call you."

"Oh, Jesus. We're supposed to be meeting people in the city tonight. I'm already in Manhattan."

I wasn't exactly sure what Mara expected me to do. Maybe she thought I, like Superman, could stop the world from spinning on its axis and reverse time, thereby enabling my father to catch an early plane out of San Francisco. Unfortunately, Cinderella's powers are limited to serving meals and snagging princes.

Through the phone, I could hear a horn honk. "Okay, okay," she muttered. I heard some more honking. Even when she's not distracted and talking on her cell phone, Mara's not exactly the most focused driver.

"Listen," she said. "I'm going to try the girls. If you see them, will you let them know the situation? Tell them your dad can't drive them to their dad's and they should just call a cab or call their dad to pick them up?" She continued to think out loud for another few minutes, going through the logistics of her night. I just sat there eating my chicken nuggets, not saying anything, like she was a character on a TV show I was too lazy to get up and turn off.

"Well, okay, you have fun tonight," she said, finally

remembering she was actually talking to someone.

"Thanks," I said.

"What's that?" she shouted over the sudden static. "I"m losing you, Lucy."

"I said *thanks*," I repeated, louder this time.

"I can't hear you, Lucy," she said. Then, "Lucy? Lucy?" Then silence.

No sooner had I hung up the phone than the front door flew open and slammed shut. I heard a cell phone ringing, but it wasn't mine. I returned to eating my nuggets.

"Hello? Hello?" Princess One appeared in the doorway of the kitchen, cell phone pressed to her ear. She dropped her backpack onto a chair. "Mom, is that you?" She listened for a second before shaking her head and hanging up.

"I think that was Mom," she said over her shoulder. "But I have, like, no idea what she said." Princess Two materialized by her sister's side.

"I think she was telling you my dad's flight's trapped in San Francisco, she's in the city, she's going out for dinner, you're supposed to call a cab or ask your dad to pick you up."

"*WHAT?*" Princess One screamed. She stared at me openmouthed, then grabbed her sister by the arm.

"What?" I repeated. Was she really that freaked out about the change of plans?

"What?" Princess Two asked.

Princess One was still clutching her sister. "Did you *hear* that?"

"Hear what?"

Princess One turned to her sister and spoke very slowly. "Mom said Doug can't drive us to dad's and we have to take a cab."

"So?" asked Princess Two.

"So we can go to the—" Princess One made fists of frustration as her sister continued to stare at her blankly. Then she leaned over and whispered something in her ear.

"OHMYGOD!" said Princess Two, just as her phone started ringing. She put it up to her ear. "Hello? . . . Oh, hi, Mom. . . . Yeah, we got your message. . . . Sure . . . Yeah, we'll just take a cab." She jumped up and down, screaming silently. "No, you don't have to call him. Really, Mom, don't worry about it." She was trying hard not to laugh at something her mother said. "Okay. . . . Okay. . . . I love you, too." She hung up and turned to her sister. "Oh. My. God. Let's go."

Even without a degree in child development, you could tell the Princesses were up to no good. I wasn't sure what I was supposed to do. I mean, it wasn't like I was some kind of authority figure. Still, if they were about to do something really stupid, maybe they could use some adult intervention. Or at least some pre-adult intervention.

"What's up?" I asked. I tried to keep my voice light, as if I just wanted to chat. "Big date tonight?"

"Wouldn't you like to know, Lucy?" asked Princess One, turning on her heel and flouncing out of the kitchen. Her sister followed with an equally indignant flounce. "Get a life, Lucy," Princess One called over her shoulder.

Ever since attending Jason Goldberg's *QM Two* extravaganza, the Princesses had been complaining there were no good bat-mitzvah party themes left, but their parting shot gave me an idea for one.

Something wicked this way comes . . .

I'd have to remember to suggest it.

When Connor picked me up to go to Piazzolla's, he was in a really bad mood. Apparently his car was in the shop again, and his parents blamed him for not taking good enough care of it.

"Like I *want* to be driving this piece of crap," he said, hitting the dashboard of the Lexus.

I didn't say much for the whole ride to Piazzolla's besides, "Mmmmhmmm" and "Yeah" and "Really?" As we pulled into the parking lot across from Piazzolla's, Connor finally said, "But enough of my bitching. How's by you, Red?"

Just as I opened my mouth to say something, he gave a shout. "Oh, yeah! A spot!" And a second later he was explaining why the Lexus was easier to park than his SUV. By the time we were out of the car and crossing the street, we'd gotten back on the subject of his parents.

"Oh my god," said Madison, waving us over to the table where she, Matt, Jessica, and Dave were already sitting. "You *have* to hear about the bags my mom saw at a store in SoHo. They're insanely cute. I think we should each get one for prom."

"Great," I said. Suddenly I had an idea. "Wait, you know what we should do?"

"What?" asked Madison, leaning toward me.

Connor, Matt, and Dave were deep in conversation, but I pulled on Connor's sleeve to get his attention. "Do you want to all go into the city tomorrow? We could get the bags, and then there's this cool Andy Goldsworthy exhibit at the Met. It's on the roof." I couldn't believe how brilliant my idea was. How perfect would it be to see the Goldsworthy exhibit with people who didn't spend our time together ignoring me?

A silence fell over the table. For almost a full minute, nobody said anything.

"I'm not really the museum type, Red," said Connor finally. "But I bet you can answer this. Dave says LeBron James played high school in Cleveland. That's not right, is it?"

Was this Connor's not-so-subtle way of telling me to drop the museum talk? "Akron," I said. "The Cavaliers drafted him out of Akron."

"Totally!" said Matt. He turned and pointed at Dave. "Who's a *loosa*!"

Connor laughed. "That's right," he said, slipping his

arm around my shoulders. "Is my girl great, or is my girl great?" Then he leaned over and made a big show of kissing me. Everyone was watching, so I kissed him back, but something was definitely wrong.

Instead of feeling like the luckiest girl in the world, I felt like a well-trained dog who'd just won best in show.

Chapter Twenty-four

As I walked from Connor's car to my front door, I was glad I'd told him I thought I was coming down with something, so he'd better not kiss me good night. What if his good night kiss made me feel like his earlier kiss had, only this time it was just the two of us there, and I couldn't blame it on our having an audience? My stomach hurt, and all I wanted to do was get into bed and stay there. Maybe I really *was* getting sick. I put my hand to my forehead. Did it feel a little warm? Probably all I needed was a cup of hot tea. I went into the kitchen to make some. The light on the answering machine was blinking.

"Hey, guys." It was my dad. "The good news is, I'm about to board a plane to Chicago. The bad news is, that's where I may be spending the night. I'll be home tomorrow late morningish. Early afternoon. Somewhere in there." The second message was from the Princesses' dad. "Hi, girls, it's Dad. I got your message. I don't know why you're not answering your cells. Anyway, tomorrow's fine. But your mom's going to have to drop you off because I have a squash game. All right. Sleep well."

Well, well, well. So the little Princesses *were* up to no good. I took some Mint Medley out of the cupboard, wondering where they'd gone. Maybe on a date? Or to a boy-girl party? I pictured a bunch of seventh graders at the movies or playing spin the bottle. It was kind of cute, actually.

My cell started ringing, and I reached into my bag. But it wasn't there. I felt around frantically. Where was my cell? The ringing stopped. I dug through the pockets of Connor's jacket. Hadn't I taken it with me when I left the house?

Just as I was about to call the number myself, it started ringing again. I listened for a second, then opened the freezer. There, next to the chicken nuggets, was my phone. I grabbed it, noticing that in addition to having a Popsicle for a cell, I had four missed calls.

"Hello?"

"Lucy?" It sounded like more than one person was saying my name.

"Who is this?" I asked.

"Lucy? Is that you?" There were two distinct voices, both of them speaking just above a whisper.

"This is Lucy," I said. I spoke very clearly and

loudly, like I needed to compensate for their whispering. "Who is—"

"Lucy, you have to come get us!" said one of the voices. And now that she was speaking solo, I knew who it was.

"Emma?" I asked.

"Lucy, come get us, please," she said.

"Please, Lucy, will you come and get us?" echoed Amy.

"Where *are* you?" I put my hand over my ear, as if the reason I was having trouble hearing the Princesses was the silent house I was standing in.

"We're at . . ." there was a muffled conversation between them and then a pause.

"Where *are* you?" I repeated.

"We're at Bobby's house," said Amy.

"Eighteen Mill Road," said Emma.

"But what are you doing *there*?" I demanded. "You're supposed to be at your *dad's*."

"We came to the . . . to the . . ." Amy started to cry, and I heard Emma say, "Give me the phone." Then there was another pause, and finally Emma's voice came on the line.

"We're at a party," she said, and her voice started to waver, too. "We're scared, Lucy," said Emma. Now she was crying, too. As much as I disliked my stepsisters, it was terrible to hear them crying like that.

"Look, just call your dad and tell him to come

get you. He can probably be there in, like, five minutes."

"We . . . we . . . can't." Emma started crying harder. Amy got back on the phone.

"If we call Dad, we'll get in trouble. We're not supposed to be here."

"Why don't you just call a cab and come home, then?" I suggested.

Rather than comforting them, my suggestion sent both Emma and Amy into a fresh round of sobbing. By now all they could say was "We can't," and "We're scared," and "Lucy, please come get us." They sounded so plaintive I almost forgot how annoying they usually are. By the third time Emma said, "We're scared, Lucy," I started to worry that maybe they really did have something to be scared about.

"Okay," I said finally. "Look, I'll come get you."

My saying that only made them cry harder, though in between sobs one or the other of them managed to say "Thank you, Lucy" a few times.

"Look, just stay where you are," I said. "I'll be there as fast as I can."

I hung up and dialed the Glen Lake Cab Company.

Eighteen Mill Road turned out to be a Tudor-style mansion set way back from the road. An enormous beech tree with gnarled branches towered over the front lawn, and I felt a flicker of anxiety as the cab turned into the circular driveway and pulled up to the dark, creepy house. What if the girls were in some kind of trouble that I couldn't handle? I told the driver I'd be right out and asked him to wait.

I tried to see in one of the small side windows by the front door, but in addition to being about seven feet off the ground, it was stained glass. I rang the bell. No response. And again. It took three more rings before a voice finally asked, "Who is it?"

I squeezed my hands into fists. This was it. "Open the door," I said firmly. Nothing happened for a few seconds, and then the door swung open.

Standing before me was a skinny boy in baggy jeans who couldn't have been more than thirteen. Seeing him made me feel ridiculous for having been scared about what I'd find in the house, but seeing me obviously didn't have the same effect on him. His face grew instantly paler. He held the door, nervously toying with the lock.

"I've come to get Emma and Amy," I said. My voice sounded parental even to me, and the boy stepped aside to let me pass.

"I think they're in the back," he said.

"Fine." I started to walk past him authoritatively before I realized I didn't actually know how to get to "the back." A hallway branched off to the left, and I followed the sound of pulsating rap until I found myself in a dimly lit room.

The air was thick with smoke. Empty bottles were scattered around the floor along with what looked like shards from a broken glass. On the sofa a girl was sitting on a guy's lap, kissing him. Her legs were around his waist, and his hands were up the back of her shirt. In the corner, three guys and a girl sat around a glass-topped table on which a ball of tin foil sat beside a razor blade. The whole thing was so gross I felt sick. Was this what seventh graders were doing for fun nowadays? What was wrong with a little spin the bottle?

Baggy Jeans came up behind me.

"We're just—" he started to say.

I held up my hand to stop him. "Save it," I said. "I don't want to know." He jiggled some loose change in his pocket nervously. "Just find my sisters and tell them to meet me by the front door."

When Emma and Amy met me in the entryway, they wouldn't look me in the eye. "See you, Bobby," they said as we stepped outside.

"Yeah, see you," he said, closing the door and locking it.

"Hi," I said as soon as we were alone. Neither of them said anything; they just examined the gravel at their feet. "Are you okay?" I asked finally.

They nodded, still not looking up.

Finally Emma spoke. "It wasn't supposed to be like that," she said. "It wasn't supposed to be just eighth graders." Instead of looking at me, she stared at the cab.

"Those were *eighth* graders?"

Amy winced, misunderstanding my tone. "Are you mad at us?" she asked.

I said. "I'm mad at *them.*" I turned toward the house. "They're all such . . ." But remembering how Emma and Amy had cried into the phone earlier made me doubt they were in need of a major anti-drug lecture. Maybe this was one of those times to leave well enough alone. "I'm not mad at you," I said firmly. "And I'm glad you called me."

"Thanks, Lucy," Amy said. Suddenly she took a step toward me and threw her arms around my waist. A second later, Emma did the same.

"We thought you'd be really mad," Emma explained.

"But we didn't know what to do," Amy added. "We didn't know who to call."

"Then we thought of you," Emma said. "We left you like a million messages."

"And then you answered." They both still had their arms around me. When I tried to walk, I felt like I was in a three-legged race.

Chapter Twenty-five

It had been a long time since I'd woken up on a Saturday morning without one of Connor's perfect kisses from the night before running through my mind. But instead of thinking about his imperfect kiss, I found myself thinking about Emma and Amy. I was in shock—they had been so . . . nice. Right before they went upstairs to bed, they'd each given me a huge hug, and Emma had said, "You're the best, Lucy." Then Amy said, "Yeah, Lucy. We're so lucky to have you as a big sister."

I got out of bed, brushed my teeth, threw on some jeans and a T-shirt, and headed to the kitchen, actually looking forward to breakfast with my family.

The first thing I heard when I pushed open the door of the basement was Emma and Amy's dad. "The only lesson you'll learn from *that* is how you can get away with doing whatever you want."

I stepped into the kitchen. Mara was standing up, leaning against the sink. Emma, Amy, and their dad were sitting at the kitchen table, Emma and Amy on one side, their dad on the other. Mr. Gilman was wearing white shorts and a white-collared shirt, and as he sat there he bounced a racket against his knee.

Emma's face was tear streaked. "No, Daddy, that's not true," she said.

You didn't have to be psychic to put two and two together. I wanted to help, but it occurred to me that maybe the story they'd told their parents diverged from the truth; the last thing they needed was me "defending" them by blurting out salient details they'd chosen to omit. I nodded hello to Mr. Gilman, went over to the fridge, and took out the orange juice.

"Lucy, I'd like to talk to you about this," said Mara. "The whole thing is quite upsetting to me."

I looked toward my stepsisters, but their eyes were down. I felt really bad for them. "Well, I know it's none of my business, but I think you should go easy on them." I walked over to the cabinet and got a glass. "They had kind of a rough night."

"That's very generous of you," said Mara. "But I think Amy and Emma need to pay for what they've done. And I'd like to know more about the role you played in their little . . . adventure."

I put the glass and the container down, totally confused. Why did I suddenly feel like a suspect on *CSI: Long Island*?

"I don't quite follow you," I said.

"The girls told me you knew they were at the party," said Mara.

I was sure I must have misheard her. "Excuse me?!"

She repeated herself, carefully enunciating each syllable. "They said you knew they were at the party. Apparently you even picked them up in a cab when it was over."

I looked down at my stepsisters. Clearly they'd decided trouble is like a pie—the bigger my piece, the smaller theirs.

"Are you implying that's *not* what happened?" Mara asked. She tried to make it sound like she actually cared about my answer, which was a total joke. No way was she entertaining the possibility that her precious angels were lying through their teeth.

It was a good thing I'd put the glass down on the table because if I hadn't, I might have thrown it at her. Was it only a few minutes ago that I'd been happy about the prospect of a meal with my family? Now I had the urge to leap across the room and strangle all of them—Mara, Emma, and Amy. No, wait. Maybe what I should do was strangle my stepsisters, then rip one of Mara's expensive Italian leather boots off her foot and drive the heel like a spike right through her heart.

The refrigerator clicked on in the silence. As its engine whirred, I picked up the juice glass, put it back into the cabinet, walked over to the fridge, and put the juice away. The whole time, nobody said a word.

When I got to the basement door, I turned and faced my stepmother. "You know what, Mara? I'm not implying anything."

I opened the door to my dungeon and pulled it shut behind me.

It was almost noon by the time the cab pulled up and I heard my dad walking into the house. "Hello?" he called. "Hello, anybody home?" Mara answered him, but I didn't. I just lay on my bed, listening to Roxy Music on my iPod and thinking about how mad I was.

How mad I was at him.

It didn't take long before there was a knock at my door.

"Lucy?"

"Yeah?"

He opened the door and started downstairs.

"Lucy, I need to talk with you," he said, his foot hitting the bottom step. His voice sounded tired, and I remembered he'd spent most of the night in an airport.

"I don't really feel like talking, Dad," I said. I didn't sit up, and I didn't take off my headphones. For a second I let myself enjoy the insane fantasy that he wasn't coming to talk to me about what had happened with Emma and Amy, he was coming to talk to me about something completely different. *Lucy, last night at O'Hare I had an epiphany. What a nightmare you've been living. I am so incredibly sorry for everything I've put you through, and I hope you can forgive me. Mara and I are getting a divorce. You and I are moving back to San Francisco. Please pack up your stuff and be ready to leave for the airport in an hour.*

"Lucy, this is all very upsetting to me. What exactly happened last night?"

I sat up. "What is it you'd like to know, *exactly*?"

He seemed surprised by my answer, or maybe it was just my tone. Either way, he hesitated for a second before saying, "Well . . . I guess I'd like to know what's going on."

I took my earphones out. "Really, Dad? Would you *really* like to know what's going on?"

He shook his head from side to side, already annoyed. "Lucy, you—"

"Okay, Dad, why don't I tell you what's going on. Here's what's going on. You get married. You move me out here, you leave me with these people I barely know, you act like we're all supposed to magically become this family, and then you run back to San Francisco so you can get to work on your 'big case.' So you can get to be the happy, bi-coastal newlywed who doesn't have to give up the biggest, greatest, most important, most fabulous, most incredible, most important, most mind-boggling case in the universe. You just *dump* me here and—"

"Lucy, I didn't *dump* you here. You live here. This is your—"

242

"Oh, wait, wait, wait!" I said, waving my arms. "Let me guess. Um . . ." I put my hand up to my forehead and closed my eyes, like a game-show contestant who just needs a few seconds more to think of the right answer. "It's my . . . home. Right? Am I right, Dad?" I nodded my head with fake enthusiasm.

He crossed his arms and leaned against the banister. "Lucy, I thought we'd talked about how sarcasm isn't really helpful."

"Oh really, Dad? Then you tell me. What's helpful? What's helpful, Dad? Because let me tell you something. This is not my home." I pointed at him. "*You're* my home. *You*, Dad. Not Mara. Not Emma and Amy. *You*. Or you were. But I guess I don't really have a home anymore, now do I? And I guess that's not all that important to you, is it? That's just not as big a deal as your great big case." I stared at him for a long minute, and then I lay back down and felt around the bed for my headphones.

For a long beat, my dad was quiet, and then he said, "Lucy, it's—"

"You know what, Dad, I really don't feel like talking to you anymore. So if you don't mind, could you please leave me alone?" I slipped my earphones back on and turned up the volume as loud as I could stand it.

My dad didn't move, and I closed my eyes. When I opened them, he was gone.

Chapter Twenty-six

I spent almost the whole weekend downstairs, sleeping or pretending to be asleep, not bothering to pick up my cell when it rang or to check my voice mail. The last thing I could deal with was telling Connor, Jessica, and Madison that I'd chosen the week before prom to tell my dad off in a way that guaranteed I'd be grounded for life. When I heard my dad and Mara go out for dinner Saturday night, I went upstairs and made a peanut-butter sandwich, then grabbed two bags of baby carrots and a box of Muslix to see me through. Sunday afternoon, Emma and Amy's dad dropped them off; later one or both of them knocked at my door, but I didn't respond.

I got up early Monday morning; the house was quiet and my dad's briefcase was still in the downstairs hallway, which was unusual but not unprecedented. Once in a while he flew out to California on Monday morning instead of Sunday evening. How ironic—the first time in months he was around for an extra night and we weren't speaking to each other.

At lunch on my way to the studio, I ran into Connor. "Yo, Red," he said. "Why didn't you call me back?" He slung his arm around my shoulder and started walking me in the same direction he'd been headed.

"Oh, god," I said. "I was having the worst weekend." It felt really nice to have Connor's arm around me as we walked together.

"That sucks, Red," he said. "You want to come to the gym with me?" He mimed lifting a set of free weights. "You know—root for the home team." He adopted the posture of a bodybuilder posing for admirers. "Me and Dave and Matt are gonna lift for a while. It'll be so much cooler if you're there."

Connor circled me, dribbling an imaginary basketball. "And he moves it up the court. He sets up the shot. He scores!" Connor threw his hands over his head, victorious, and made the sound of a crowd cheering wildly.

"Nice one," I said.

"Thanks, Red," he said, coming up behind me and wrapping his arms around my waist.

It felt so good to stand there with Connor holding me. It was like the whole horrible fight with my family hadn't even happened. He nuzzled the back of my neck.

"I missed you, Red," he said.

And right then and there, I made a decision. Even if

my dad grounded me, I was going to the prom. If I had to run away and live out the rest of my days on the streets, so be it. Connor was taking some other girl over my dead body.

I turned around and we kissed. "I missed you, too," I said, when we finally came up for air. Had I really been grossed out by his kiss Friday night? Clearly my brain had experienced exposure to some toxic chemical or something.

I went in for another kiss.

"Mmm, nice," he said, pulling away. "So you gonna come to the gym?"

Watching Connor, Dave, and Matt lift weights didn't exactly sound like the most exciting way to spend a period, but Connor was the only bright spot in my otherwise dismal life. If he wanted me to watch him work out, I'd watch him work out.

"Let me just finish this one thing," I said. My landscape was going about a million times faster than my self-portrait ever had, but I was still behind since I'd started on it so late. I'd sworn to Ms. Daniels that I'd have it finished by the end of the week, and one section was proving almost impossible to get right. "Give me twenty minutes."

"You know it," he said, backing away. God, he was handsome; I could still feel his lips on mine. "Be there or be square."

Sam was leaving the studio as I was walking in, and since

I was in my usual post-Connor-kiss haze, I barreled right into him.

"You know, art is not normally a contact sport," he said.

"I'm really sorry," I said. Clearly Connor needed his own warning label: DO NOT ATTEMPT TO RESUME NORMAL ACTIVITY WITHIN FIVE MINUTES OF KISSING THIS PERSON.

"No, it was all me," said Sam. "I'm running late."

I bent down and picked up the pen he'd dropped on the floor when we collided. "For a very important date?"

"Thanks," he said, taking the pen and slipping it into his back pocket. "For a very *unpleasant* date, actually. I've got to get my tux."

I remembered how much fun Madison and Jessica and I'd had shopping for our dresses. "That'll be great," I said, smiling both at the memory and my recent decision to go to the prom no matter the consequences. "You'll probably really like it."

"Actually, I probably really won't," he said. Then he laughed, but it sounded forced. "Sorry, don't let me rain on your prom parade." He patted me on the shoulder and started down the corridor. "See ya."

"See ya," I called after him.

The studio was totally empty. I set up my easel and started working, focusing on the tiny corner of the canvas that had been giving me trouble. The green I'd mixed looked good, and I smeared it a little with a sponge. Then I dipped my brush into some blue and swirled a small line in the green.

Yeah. I blotted the edges until the blue was a fuzzy shadow on the grass. Perfect. Dip, swirl, blot. Dip, swirl, blot.

When I looked up at the clock, half an hour had passed. Damn. I totally hadn't meant to keep Connor waiting. I put my painting away and pushed the easel back against the wall as fast as I could, then brought my brush over to the sink to wash it. Of course the paint took forever to come out; no matter how hard I scrubbed at the bristles, the water refused to run clear. Just as I started to get really stressed out about how long everything was taking, I noticed that the rich blue running down the drain was almost the exact same color as my prom dress. Like Connor was going to remember I'd once been ten minutes late to meet him at the gym when he saw me in that dress. The dress. I pictured my dress, pictured myself wearing it as I floated across the dance floor toward a tux-clad Connor. How awesome was it going to be to feel his arms around me as we slow danced the night away? Connor and Lucy at the prom. I closed my eyes to better see the image.

A second later my eyes flew open. My heart was pounding and I couldn't catch my breath. I'd just done what Madison told me to do at Roses are Red—pictured myself at prom, having the most romantic time of my life, slow dancing with my perfect prince.

The only problem was, in my picture, I wasn't dancing with Connor.

I was dancing with Sam.

Chapter Twenty-seven

The CD Jessica had burned for me may have successfully drowned out the sounds of dinner being served, but it couldn't do anything about the delicious smells wafting downstairs.

Chinese take-out.

I couldn't believe it. We *never* got Chinese food. Mention Chinese food in front of my stepmother and she'd go on for hours about sodium content, fatty oils, MSG. When my dad and I lived in San Francisco, we probably ate Chinese twice a week. Since moving to New York ten months ago, we'd had it three times. Each time, Mara had been out for the evening.

I felt like a guerilla warrior hiding in the jungle. They could do what they wanted, but no way were they going to smoke me out. The baby carrots I'd stashed in my room over the weekend were all gone. I turned up the volume on my iPod. Who needs food when you have Janis Joplin? I sang a few lines out loud. "Summertime, and the living is easy. Fish are jumping, and the cotton is high."

I definitely smelled orange chicken, my all-time favorite dish. In San Francisco, there was a place that made it perfectly—crunchy skin outside, tender chicken inside, lots of caramelized orange peel. Two of the three restaurants we'd tried on Long Island made it kind of chewy and bland, but the third really knew what they were doing. My mouth filled with saliva, and I swallowed. The song ended, and the prom song came on.

Prom. Connor. Sam. I snapped off the music and rolled over, burying my face in my pillow.

Why isn't there an OFF button for your brain?

I felt dizzy, whether from hunger or my thoughts I wasn't sure. Either way, I couldn't just stay where I was. I decided that since Mara, Emma, and Amy were definitely eating in the dining room, I'd go upstairs, serve myself some food, eat it alone in the kitchen, and then watch the basketball game in the den. The only thing worse than eating and watching a game by yourself is starving and not watching a game by yourself. I headed up.

When I pushed open the door, I was greeted by the single most shocking sight of my life. Not only were Emma, Amy, and Mara eating around the kitchen table (something Mara says only servants should do), but my *dad* was sitting there with them.

"I thought we might be able to lure you up here," he said, nodding at the table piled high with takeout containers.

I looked from one of them to the other, trying to figure out what, exactly, was going on. Emma and Amy were sitting facing my dad and Mara, their backs to me.

This was not part of my plan. It was one thing to sneak some food out of a container while my wicked stepmother and her evil daughters comparison shopped through *Lucky* in the dining room. It was another to fill my plate up and sit at the counter by myself while everyone else sat there watching me. My hand was still on the doorknob. Was it too late to turn around and head back downstairs? I remembered a special report I heard on the news once that said it's important to have a three-day supply of food and water on hand at all times. Why hadn't I taken that broadcast more seriously?

My dad pointed at an unopened container with his chopsticks. "Orange chicken," he said.

Okay, this was completely unfair. I mean, I was starving.

"Why don't you come sit with us?" asked my dad. He pulled out the chair next to him and patted the seat.

Without removing my hand from the doorknob, I considered my options. A) Turn around, go back downstairs, potentially starve to death or B) Sit down, eat, watch basketball game.

But if I sat down and ate with them, would I be

expected to *talk* to them? I looked at Emma's and Amy's backs, remembered their frantic phone call, the rescue. *Thank you, Lucy. We love you, Lucy. Lucy, you're the best.*

Traitors.

I decided I'd sit and eat but not speak. I walked over to the chair my dad had pulled out and sat down. Mara passed me the container of orange chicken. I unfolded the foil edges and took off the plastic top. Everyone was looking at me as if I'd just had a miraculous recovery from a deadly illness. I served myself some chicken and took a bite. It was hard to swallow with four sets of eyes watching my every move. When I put my fork down, Emma reached across the table to hand me a container.

"Rice?"

I nodded. A nod does not equal a spoken word. I spooned some rice onto my plate while everyone else sat in silence. I took another bite.

"Emma and Amy have something they would like to say to you," said my dad.

I looked across the table at Emma and Amy, my mouth full of orange chicken. Their heads were bent.

"Girls," said my dad.

Emma looked up. After a second, Amy did, too. "We're sorry, Lucy," they said in stereo.

I swallowed, but I didn't say anything. There was a silence, and then my dad prodded them again. "Sorry for what?"

"We're sorry we got you in trouble," said Emma, dropping her head down.

"We're sorry we made it sound like you knew we were at the party the whole time," said Amy, whose head was now also down.

Suddenly Emma looked up. "Really, we're sorry," she said. "You were so nice, Lucy."

"Don't hate us, Lucy," said Amy.

I wasn't sure what to say. I mean, I didn't exactly hate them. But I didn't exactly trust them, either. I looked around the table. My dad took a bite of his moo-shu pancake, and I thought I caught a glance pass between him and Mara.

"Lucy, now it's my turn to apologize," said Mara. "I should have trusted you wouldn't have done something to endanger Emma and Amy."

Were we in an alternate universe? I nodded at her. She grabbed a paper napkin from the pile next to her and handed it to me. "Here," she said. "For your lap."

So we *were* in the real world. "Thanks," I said, taking it.

Nobody said much for the rest of the meal. When we finished eating, my dad brought over the big kitchen garbage can and we dumped all the paper plates and empty containers and disposable chopsticks into it.

I was pretty sure it was the first time since San Francisco that I hadn't been asked to clear the table.

* * *

Later my dad came downstairs just as I was setting my alarm.

"Hey," he said.

"Hey," I said. I checked the volume and made sure it was set to go off in the A.M., not the P.M.

"So I'm going to work out of the New York office for the next couple of weeks," he said, leaning over the banister. "Like I did today."

I put the clock back down on the floor next to my bed. "Sure," I said.

"That's the best I can do for now."

"Okay," I said.

He waited, like he wanted to say something else. Or maybe he was waiting for me to say something else, I wasn't sure. But what was I supposed to say? *I guess everything's okay now. Emma and Amy said they're sorry, you temporarily relocated to New York, and Mara let us have Chinese food and eat in the kitchen! Bibbitybobbityboo!—we're one big happy family.*

As it was, my dad and I just ended up looking at each other in silence for a while.

"So I guess I'll see you tomorrow," he said.

"Yeah," I said.

"Well," he said, "good night."

"Good night."

It took me forever to fall asleep.

What my dad had said made it impossible for me

to stop thinking about how my life would change if he really was working in his firm's New York office instead of flying out to the West Coast every Sunday. The idea of him opening the front door each night when he got home from work made me so happy I almost started crying. How easy would it be to sit through dinner with my step-monster and her offspring if my dad was there, too; if afterward he and I watched a game together or went for ice cream like we used to? If he was around, wasn't it possible my home life would actually become . . . bearable?

Finally I made myself roll over and go to sleep. Because while my fantasy was certainly a nice one, the reality wasn't so pretty. "Two weeks," I said into my pillow. "He said two weeks."

That's the problem with fairy tales. Every good thing happens for a limited time only.

Chapter Twenty-eight

All week prom gossip flew fast and furious. In math, while Mr. Palmer droned on about graphing parabolas, I taught Jessica what a point spread was, using the latest rumors about which couples would make it to Saturday night and which wouldn't. Even though I was doing it while he was talking about something else, I thought Mr. Palmer would have been proud to hear me explain, when we got to Jane and Sam, that you can't solve an equation if you don't know whether something (i.e., Jane's bitchiness) is a variable or a constant. I realized that despite my math teacher's being clinically insane, I'd actually learned something in his class.

Having just been talking about him in math, I was surprised when Sam didn't show up to art, and I was even more surprised when he wasn't there the next day, either. It wasn't until the end of the week that

I asked Ms. Daniels where he was, and while she was telling me all about the colleges he was visiting and how she hoped he'd seriously consider RISD, I suddenly remembered the daydream I'd had about us slow dancing at the prom. It made me feel really self-conscious. First I have a weird vision of us dancing together and then I'm all concerned about why he isn't in school? Just as I was starting to seriously regret having bothered to ask Ms. Daniels about Sam's whereabouts, I saw Jessica and Madison standing in the open door of the studio. Jessica pointed at her watch and I cut Ms. Daniels off, explaining that I had to run.

My worrying about why I was worrying about why Sam was absent didn't last very long. By the time we were halfway down the hall and I'd heard Jessica's new-and-improved unofficial polling data indicating that Connor and I were definitely going to be prom king and queen, I barely remembered I'd been talking to Ms. Daniels, much less what we'd been talking about.

Meanwhile, having my dad at home was almost the sugar-coated fantasy I'd spun in my imagination.

Almost.

As I'd hoped, we watched a game together and we went for ice cream (well, gelato). And it wasn't Mara interrupting the game so my dad could look at fabric samples for the chair in their bedroom or Emma and Amy coming with us on our dessert run that made his being home less than perfect. It was the big red X's I kept drawing on my mental calendar. Thirteen. Eleven. Ten.

Because even while I wanted to celebrate the fact that I'd gotten my father back, I couldn't help measuring how happy I was now against how bad I was going to feel when he left again for San Francisco.

The morning of the prom I woke up to my cell ringing. I could tell from the light managing to fight its way through the tiny basement windows that it was going to be a beautiful sunny day.

"We're meeting at Madison's at four, right?" It was Jessica.

"Yeah, right," I said, yawning. "Four o'clock."

"I told Kathryn she should come over, too," said Jessica. "To get ready and everything."

Only half awake, I wondered if I'd heard Jessica right. "Kathryn? I thought she wasn't coming."

"Oh, yeah, well, she and her boyfriend had this mondo fight last night. She's coming *stag*." Jessica laughed. "I said she could come in our limo. Isn't that cool?"

"Ah, yeah, it's pretty cool."

Is it still called going stag if your plan is to arrive alone but leave with someone else's date?

"So you'll be here at four, right?" Jessica asked.

"Right," I said. "I'll be there at four."

My dad and Mara were gone when I got upstairs.

There was a note. GONE ANTIQUING. Of course. *Of course.* Hadn't I known it was only a matter of time before we went back to business as usual? Probably they'd forgotten about the prom, too, forgotten I needed to be at Madison's at four. Good thing I had the Glen Lake cab company on speed dial.

At three o'clock, just as I was getting out of the shower, I heard my dad's car pull up in the driveway. A few minutes later there was a knock on my door.

"Yeah?" I had an open bag on my bed full of stuff for the prom and the Hamptons.

"Lucy? Can we come down?"

"Fine."

The door opened and my dad and Mara came down. Or started coming down. It seemed to be taking them forever. I looked over to the stairs and saw they were each carrying a heavy bundle wrapped in brown paper. They must have been heading to the basement storage area to put away whatever precious treasures they'd discovered along the Hudson River.

"Hey," said my dad when he got to the bottom step. He was panting slightly. Mara was standing behind him, but thanks to her daily gym sessions, she wasn't out of breath.

"Hey," I said.

We stood there for another minute. "We were up in Lomax today," said my dad.

"Oh." Just how many breakfronts does one household need?

My dad was smiling at me. "I remembered you'd admired this, so we wanted to get it for you."

I wasn't sure what he was talking about. "This?" I asked.

He pointed at the package Mara held balanced against her hip. "Open it."

I went over to Mara and took the package from her. Kneeling down in front of it, I pulled at the brown paper, ripping off one layer after another. I wondered if it was going to turn out to be one of those tiny little boxes that's inside a dozen bigger containers. God, she'd probably gotten me some terrible piece of jewelry to wear for the prom. *Lucy, the bad news is I haven't been able to furnish your room. The good news is I've been able to furnish you! With this lovely rhinestone pendant featuring a Pilates instructor and her pupil.*

Finally I hit something that wasn't brown paper, and all at once I knew what was underneath the wrapping I'd been wrestling with.

"Oh my god," I said. I tore off a section of paper to reveal a leg of the wooden easel I'd seen so long ago. "Wow." I studied the claw-feet and traced my hand along the intricate woodwork. It was even more beautiful than I'd remembered, or maybe it had just been polished. Even in the dim light, the wood gleamed. "Thanks," I said, standing up.

"We thought . . . well, I thought." My dad cleared his throat, still struggling to find the right pronoun. "It seemed possible you might like to put this on it." He walked toward me, awkwardly balancing the large, square package he was holding. "I was supposed to save it for your eighteenth birthday," he said, "but I thought you could use it now." He lay it at my feet and took a step back.

"Oh," I said. "What is it?"

My dad paused and swallowed. "It's a painting your mother did. She wanted you to have it."

The three of us stood there, not moving or saying anything, as if the brown rectangle at my feet was ticking. After a minute my dad put his hand on Mara's shoulder. "Excuse me a second," she said. Then she turned and went upstairs.

My dad gave a little cough. "Do you mind if I stay while you open it?"

My throat was tight, and I just shook my head to indicate I didn't mind. Then I untied the cord and peeled back the wrapping.

I hadn't seen one of my mother's paintings in a long time—since we'd packed them up and put them in storage when we moved—and I'd never seen this one before. The painting was of a city wall covered in graffiti and posters, some of which were peeling off, some of which were partly covered over by other posters. Each of the posters was a self-portrait of my mom, the same one repeated over and over in slightly different colors—greens and blues, browns and yellows, and here and there the faint purple of shadow. Her eyes were wide, her hair wild and curly around her small face, her smile mysterious as the *Mona Lisa*'s. As my eyes studied the posters, I realized they were grouped together in order to form a composite image. Once I figured that out, it only took me a minute to see that it was of a woman holding a baby in her arms.

"She started this when she got sick," said my dad, his voice thick. "She made it for you." He lifted his hand to his face, and I realized he was crying. "She would have been so happy to know you're becoming an artist."

I'd never seen my dad cry before, and it made me start to cry, too.

"I wish I had known her," I said. "I wish she had known me." And then I added, "I wish we could have been a family."

My dad put his arm around me and squeezed my shoulders. "I wish that, too," he said, taking a deep breath and wiping his eyes with the back of his hand. "You know, Lucy goose, I can't make everything perfect. I wish I could, but I can only do the best I can. And I—" He took a deep, shuddering breath. "I'll always be your home. And you'll always be mine. And I hope that someday this will feel like your home, too."

I knew if I tried to say something, I'd start bawling.

"So here's the deal, kiddo." He dug a handkerchief

out of his pocket and blew his nose. "I'm going to be home for another week. Then I'm going back to San Francisco for two more weeks. And after that, if I can't work on things from the New York office, I told them they're going to have to finish up without me." He squeezed my shoulders. "What do you say to that?"

I opened my mouth to answer him, and a really loud sob came out. I put my hand on my mouth and shook my head.

"Is that a 'No' head shake or an 'Okay' head shake?"

I shook my head again.

"No?" said my dad.

I shook my head again.

"Okay," he said. I could tell from his voice that he was smiling.

I nodded, and he handed me his handkerchief. "It's a bit worse for wear," he said.

I blew my nose, loud, and took a deep breath. Then we sat there, not saying anything, just looking at the painting together.

Finally I wiped my eyes on my sleeve. "I guess I should get going," I said.

"I guess so," he said.

Just as I stood up, there was a pounding above our heads. Seconds later, Emma and Amy came tumbling down the stairs. "We want to see Lucy in her dress. We want to see Lucy in her dress!"

They stopped short when they saw me.

"What are you wearing?" they demanded. "Where's your dress?"

I pointed at the garment bag. "It's over there. I'm getting dressed at Madison's."

"What?" They looked at me like I'd just announced my intention to eat one of them for dinner. "But you can't! You have to get dressed here!"

"Lucy, you *have* to let us help you."

"I don't really need help getting dressed."

Emma circled around the bed. "You know what we mean."

"I'd love to see you in the dress," said my dad. "Unless that would ruin your plans."

"Yeah, Lucy," said Emma. "You put it on now."

"Yeah," echoed Amy. "Put it on."

Emma, sensing my resolve was weakening, took advantage of her opportunity. "Okay, we're going to go upstairs, and then we'll come back in five minutes, and you have the dress on." She started herding everyone upstairs in front of her. "Come *on*," she said when my dad hesitated. "Move it." Once she'd gotten everyone onto the staircase, Emma turned back to me. "Five minutes," she said.

I listened to the door shut behind the three of them, and then I walked over to the dress. I took a long time removing my jeans and my T-shirt, folding them perfectly and putting them "away" onto their respective piles on the floor. Then I slipped out of my bra and slid the garment bag off the hanger, removing the pins that, since there were no straps, were holding the dress in place. I'd barely had time to step into it and reach around to zip the bottom half of the zipper before the door to the basement flew open.

"We're coming down, Lucy," yelled Amy.

"Yeah, ready or not, here we come," yelled Emma. And in a second, they were standing next to me. My dad and Mara followed more slowly, Mara coming all the way into the basement, my dad sitting on the bottom step.

"Ooooh," said Emma.

"Mmmmm," said Amy.

"It's sooo pretty," said Emma.

"I love it," said Amy.

They circled around me, evaluating the dress from different angles.

"It's really beautiful, Lucy," said my dad.

Mara walked over to me and put her hand on my back. "May I?"

"Sure," I said, letting go of the fabric so she could zip the zipper. For a second it felt like it was going to be too tight, but she coaxed it up until it closed all the way.

"It's lovely," she said, stepping back and surveying me.

"What shoes are you wearing?" asked Emma.

"Yeah, what shoes?" asked Amy.

"Those." I pointed at my bag. The toe of one of my black pumps was sticking out the top.

"*What?*" shrieked Amy.

"Are you *crazy?*" This from Emma.

"Girls!" said my dad sharply.

"Sorry," said Emma.

"Yeah, sorry," said Amy.

"I don't have anything else," I explained. "Sorry."

Emma started jumping up and down, practically bursting with frustration. "You *have* to wear strappy shoes," she said.

"You have to wear *gold* strappy shoes," said Amy, jumping up and down with her.

Emma stopped jumping and made a face of disgust at Amy. "She's not wearing gold shoes," she said. "Do you live in a trailer or something? *Silver*. She has to wear *silver* sandals."

Before Amy could respond, I stepped in. "Well, guess what, ladies, I hate to break it to you, but *she*'s not wearing gold *or* silver. It's black pumps or barefoot." I found myself looking over at my dad for confirmation of my decision.

He shrugged. "Those shoes look nice to me." If my dad hadn't once paired a plaid sports jacket with striped pants, his assessment of my footwear would have been much more comforting.

And then suddenly, out of nowhere, just as I was wondering if maybe going barefoot wasn't the solution to my whole problem, Mara said, "Did you *want* silver shoes to wear?"

"Yes!" Emma and Amy shouted.

I shrugged. "Why, do you have a magic wand?"

"Not exactly," she said. "But I do have a pair of silver shoes in my closet."

By the time we arrived at Madison's, her driveway was filled with cars, and cars lined the street in front of the house. I tried just saying good-bye to my dad, Mara, Emma, and Amy, but once Emma and Amy figured out that other people's families were staying for cocktails, they refused to leave.

The party was being held in the backyard. I saw Connor across the lawn standing with Matt and Dave. He looked really handsome in his tuxedo, so much so that I couldn't believe my mental picture of prom had produced Sam instead of him. When he saw me, he gestured that I was to stay where I was and then went into the house. A minute later he came over to where I was standing.

"Yo, baby!" he said, taking in my dress and hair. "You're looking mighty fine." He slid a corsage of white gardenias over my wrist. "Here you go, Red," he said. The flowers smelled rich and thick, and I put them up to my nose and inhaled deeply.

"Thanks," I said.

I'd planned on wearing a pearl necklace of my mom's, but Emma and Amy had convinced me it was too

Town and Country, so I had on a long necklace of crystal beads that wrapped tightly around my neck like a choker, then fell halfway down my back.

"Look," Amy had said when I was finally outfitted to her satisfaction, "something old, something new, something borrowed, something blue."

"That's a wedding, you freak," said Emma. "Not a prom."

Amy shrugged. "Whatev."

Emma and Amy had worked on my hair, helping me put it up in a high, complicated bun. They wanted me to look just like a photo they'd seen in *TeenVogue* of the Princess of Liechtenstein (though it may have been Romania—they were vague on the geographical details). Whether or not I resembled European royalty, I must have looked pretty good because Connor kept winking at me and smiling. He was winking and smiling at Madison and Jessica, too, telling them how hot they looked and how lucky Matt and Dave were.

"Hi, kids!" Kathryn shouted, waving to everyone on the lawn from the deck. I don't know if she'd been drinking upstairs at Jessica's, but she was more than a little unsteady on her extremely high heels. And while the rest of us were wearing long dresses, Kathryn's dress ("dress") was short. Very short. It was so short that, when she stopped waving and started giggling, my first thought was she was embarrassed because she'd come down without her skirt on.

Connor didn't seem to mind, though. When Kathryn crossed the lawn to say hi to us, Connor gave her the same smile he'd given me, Jessica, and Madison. When he told her how hot she looked, Kathryn laughed. "Stop," she said. "I'm blushing." Then she gave him a very unsisterly hug, and I wondered if Connor's compliment had encouraged in Kathryn the idea that *I* was the one going stag and *she* was the one with the date.

The limos began to arrive at seven.

"Come on, guys," yelled Jessica. "Let's go."

Madison started maneuvering Matt toward the front. I walked over to where my dad and Mara were talking to Connor's parents.

Mrs. Pearson extended her hand. "Hello, Lucy," she said. "It's so nice to finally meet you."

"It's nice to finally meet you, too," I said. They say nobody knows a guy like his mom, so I was tempted to ask Mrs. Pearson if she thought it was a little odd that Connor had spent most of the cocktail party trying to get Kathryn in a headlock. But before I could put the question to her, Jessica came over to me. "It's showtime," she said.

"Oh, right," I said. I turned to my dad and Mara. "Well, I guess I should get going."

My dad gave me a hug. "You look gorgeous."

"Thanks," I said. "And thanks again for the painting." I looked over his shoulder at Mara. "And thanks for the easel," I said to her. "It's really beautiful."

"I'm glad you like it," she said.

"Here, let me get a picture," said Mr. Pearson. He came over to me and my dad and placed us next to each other, putting my dad's hand on my shoulder and wrapping my arm around my dad's waist. Mara was standing a few feet away, and I could tell from the way she was watching us that she really wanted to be in the picture. I kept expecting my dad to call her over, but he didn't; he just let Mr. Pearson pose us.

It was so tempting to let her stand there.

"Okay," said Mr. Pearson. He took a few steps and turned around, training his camera on us. "One, two—"

"Wait!" I shouted.

Mr. Pearson moved the camera away from his face. "What's the matter?" he asked.

"I just need to . . . hang on a second." I stepped from under my dad's arm and went over to Mara. "Come be in the picture," I said.

"It's fine, Lucy," she said. "Why don't you just get a picture of you and your dad. I really don't mind."

She's telling you it's okay. Just take the picture without her.

I shook my head. "No, really," I said. "I'd like one of all of us." And as soon as I'd said it, I realized it wasn't even a total lie.

She and I looked at each other for a minute, and then she smiled at me. I smiled back. "Okay, then," she said.

She followed me over to where my dad was waiting, and we let Mr. Pearson arrange us so that my dad was on one side of me and Mara was on the other. Just as Mr. Pearson was about to snap the picture, there was a scream. I looked over in the direction it came from to see Emma and Amy racing across the lawn to where we were standing.

"Wait!" shouted Emma.

"We want to be in the picture," said Amy. They slid in on either side of me and put their arms around my waist.

"We did her hair," Emma said to Mrs. Pearson, who was standing next to her husband.

"Well, it's lovely," she said absently.

"*I* did her hair," said Amy. "You did her makeup."

"That is such a lie," said Emma. "I totally did her hair!"

"Oh my god, what are you talking about?" Amy stamped her foot. "You didn't even *touch* her hair."

"Girls, girls," said my dad. He put a hand on each of their shoulders and nudged them to face Mr. Pearson.

"Did so," muttered Emma.

"Did not," answered Amy.

"Let's focus here," said my dad, and I felt Emma's and Amy's arms tighten around my waist as I smiled and Mara said, "Cheese."

"One, two, three," said Mr. Pearson. And for a second after the shutter clicked we all stayed just where we were. A family.

Chapter Twenty-nine

"Whoa, dude," said Connor, as we stepped into the lobby of the Plaza. He shaded his eyes with his hand. "That's bright."

While we'd all sipped genteely at our flutes during the champagne toast at Madison's, like consuming alcohol was no big deal, as soon as we got in the limo everyone started chugging from flasks that Connor, Dave, and Matt had brought. Unfortunately one sip of whatever they were drinking was all I could handle. It burned my throat and I gasped.

"What *is* that?" I asked.

"J.D., baby," he said, tapping the flask against his chest and belching. "Your good ole friend Jack Daniel's."

We'd been warned that once we arrived at the prom, we couldn't leave, so everyone wanted to drink as much as possible on the thirty-minute drive to Manhattan.

Kathryn, who apparently *was* a good friend of Jack Daniel's, sat on Connor's left, while I sat squeezed between him and the door of the limo. The closer we got to Manhattan, the further Kathryn's dress edged up her leg and the less aware of my presence Connor seemed to be.

I don't know what I'd expected, but prom wasn't exactly turning out to be the most magical night of my life. If anything, it seemed to be like a lot of other nights. As soon as we arrived at the hotel, all the girls went into the bathroom and all the guys went into the Palm Room. It was almost as if *we'd* come together and *they'd* come together. Standing in the bathroom with Madison and Jessica, I had the strangest feeling that we weren't even at the prom; we were just in the bathroom at Piazzolla's. When we walked out, we'd be in the familiar linoleum and wood dining room, and there'd be Dave and Connor and Matt sitting at a table littered with pizza crust and crumpled paper napkins.

The table didn't have any pizza crust on it, but by the time we got there, the guys had thrown their dinner rolls at one another. Madison went ballistic, and Matt looked sheepish. We sat down, and without thinking, I took my napkin off my plate and lay it on my lap. Jessica hit Dave on the shoulder and gestured for him to put his napkin on his lap. Then we all just sat there, not saying anything.

Across the room I saw Jane come through the doorway. Her dress was bright yellow, long and tight, with a plunging neckline, and she looked gorgeous. She paused to survey her domain as Sam walked in behind her. Even though he was backlit by the bright light of the hallway, I knew it was him because his hair was standing almost straight up, like he'd been pulling on it nonstop for hours. When the door shut behind him, I saw he was wearing red Converse sneakers with his tuxedo, and I couldn't help laughing to myself, as if Sam had just told me a great joke. I began to stand up, planning to walk over and tell him I thought the sneakers were a good call, but just as I did, he put his hand on the small of Jane's back to lead her to their table.

And all of a sudden, I got a sick feeling in my stomach. Because seeing Sam guide Jane across the room, I knew. I knew. I knew why, that day in the studio, he was the person I'd imagined slow dancing with. I knew why I'd missed him when he wasn't in class this week.

Most of all, I knew why tonight felt like the least magical night of my life.

I stayed where I was, half standing, half sitting, frozen for the long minutes it took Sam and Jane to find their table. Then I forced myself to stop watching them, dropped to my seat, and took a deep breath, unable to get out from under the hot wave of sadness that had washed over me.

"They really look great together, don't they?"
"I know. I love her dress."

"It's *sooo* sexy."

Like everyone else, I had my eyes on the dance floor, where the prom king and queen were dancing. Their crowns caught the reflected rays of the twirling disco ball and sent diamonds of light around the room. Their arms were around one another, and I was trying to think if I'd ever heard of a culture where brothers and sisters danced as closely as Kathryn and Connor were dancing. Every few seconds someone whistled or yelled, "Go for it!" or just started clapping. Kathryn was clearly relishing the attention. She kept smiling and waving, and when her crown nearly slipped off, she caught it and dropped it back onto her head in a single graceful gesture without missing a step.

I could feel Madison and Jessica's concerned stares even without looking at them. From the second the prom committee chair had announced the names of the prom king and queen, they hadn't left my side, telling me how crazy the committee was, how they'd just wanted seniors to win, how Connor was totally in love with me.

"Connor's not even having a good time," Jessica said. She had her arm around me, and she squeezed my shoulder.

"I think they look really awkward together," said Madison. "She's *way* too short for him."

"Excuse me," I said. "I'm going to go to the bathroom."

"Do you want us to come?" asked Jessica.

I shook my head. "I'll be right back."

The hallway was quiet and empty. I trailed my hand along the elaborate chair rail, enjoying how my heels sank into the soft carpet.

It was the first thing I'd enjoyed all night.

Jessica and Madison couldn't have been more wrong: Kathryn and Connor looked *great* together. She'd been born to be prom queen. And he'd been born to be prom king. That they were fulfilling their destinies was undeniable.

Equally undeniable was how little jealousy I felt.

The only thing I felt was relief. Total and complete relief. I didn't want to go to the Hamptons and watch Connor and Dave and Matt get wasted. I didn't want to worry about whether or not I liked kissing Connor anymore.

And most of all, I didn't want to talk about basketball. Not now. And not for a long, long time.

The season was over. It was time to get a real life.

As I approached the corner, I heard a girl's voice. She wasn't yelling, exactly, but she was definitely pissed off.

". . . believe it when you say that."

I turned the corner. Sam and Jane were in the hallway, halfway between me and the bathroom. He was leaning against the wall, his arms crossed, and she was sitting on a low sofa across from him.

"Jane," he said, "you're not listening to me."

I stopped in my tracks. Even though my overhearing

them was a total accident, I felt sneaky, as though I'd been spying. As quickly and silently as possible, I slipped around the corner and walked back in the direction I'd come from.

Kathryn and Connor were surrounded by other couples crowding the dance floor, but because of their crowns it was still easy to spot them. Her arms were around his shoulders, and she had the fingers of one hand buried in his hair. I went over to them and tapped him on the shoulder.

"Hey, Red," he said. "How are ya'?"

"I think I'm gonna go, Connor," I said.

Connor looked at me, his eyes bloodshot. "You're leaving, Red?"

"Yeah, I just don't think I have it in me to go to the Hamptons." Kathryn didn't bother concealing the fact that she was listening, nor did she try to hide the Cheshire-cat smile my announcement elicited.

"Sure, Red," he said as they swayed back and forth to the music. "No worries."

I stood on my tiptoes and kissed him lightly on the cheek, wondering if he'd even notice that someone else would be saying *I am* when he asked, *Who's my girl?*

"See ya, Connor," I said.

"Yeah," he said, still dancing with Kathryn. "See ya."

Crossing the ballroom of the Plaza Hotel, I realized that

at school on Monday everything would be the way it had been before Connor noticed me. I could already see Jessica and Madison running off to meet Kathryn, too busy befriending Connor's new girlfriend to bother with his old one. For a second I felt sad, thinking about how lonely lunch was going to be. But then I remembered— dinner. My dad would be home for dinner. And at lunch I didn't have to sit alone in the cafeteria if I didn't want to, I could just go to the studio and work on my landscape. So maybe everything was going to be okay. Maybe in the end it was better to have an annoying stepmother and no prince than a wicked stepmother and an annoying prince.

Just before I pulled the door open, I felt a hand on my back. I turned around, Connor's name already on my lips.

"Connor, I don't—"

But it wasn't Connor. It was Sam.

"Hey," he said, slightly out of breath.

"Hey," I said.

"I just . . ." He cleared his throat and took a deep breath. "I just have to . . ." He looked at me, looked away, looked back at me. "I . . ." He laughed. "I can't believe I'm doing this." He put his hand up to his glasses and took them off. "This is going to be way easier if you're blurry." I had a second to notice how dark his eyes were before he looked away again. "Look, I know this is going to sound crazy, but the thing is, I like you." He laughed at what he'd just said. "I know that's an incredibly seventh-grade way of putting it, and I know you have a boyfriend, and I had a girlfriend up until a few minutes ago. And I know this is totally the wrong moment for everything I'm saying, but it's been on my mind for weeks, and now I'm about to leave, and if I don't say it tonight, I'm never going to get up the guts to say it again. So. I like you. And if you ever want to dump your current Prince Charming, I hope you'll consider letting me interview for the position."

WHAT?

"Sam, I—"

He popped his glasses back on his face and took a step toward the door. "Okay," he said. "Now that I have thoroughly embarrassed myself, I'm going to let you return to your fairy-tale life." He made an elaborate bow and turned to go.

"Sam, wait!" I practically had to run to catch up with him. The heel of my shoe caught on the carpet, and I would have fallen if he hadn't grabbed me.

"Whoa," he said, holding me by the elbow. "Careful."

"Sam?" I said, looking into his eyes.

"Lucy?" he said, looking straight back at me.

I took a deep breath. "Sam, let's blow this fairy tale."

He laughed uncertainly, then stopped when he saw the expression on my face. "Seriously?" he asked.

"Seriously," I said.

But as we turned to go, I realized there was one more thing I needed to do. Just because I was sure they were going to start ignoring me big-time on Monday didn't mean it was okay to leave without saying good-bye.

"Could you give me a second?"

"Sure," said Sam. "I'll meet you by the door."

I looked around, finally spotting them on the dance floor. As soon as she saw me, Madison grabbed my arm. "Hey," she said, "where were you? You weren't in the bathroom."

"Are you okay?" asked Jessica. "Connor's being a total ass." I looked past her to where Kathryn and Connor weren't dancing so much as they were standing in one place, arms around each other.

"No, he's not," I said. "I think he really likes her."

"Are you crazy?" Jessica took both my hands in hers. "He likes *you.*"

"The thing is, Jessica, he doesn't even know me." I let go of her hands since I knew the next sentence out of my mouth would probably make her want to let go of mine. "And anyway, it doesn't matter because I don't really like him."

Jessica's eyes grew enormous, and Madison clutched her hands to her chest. "You don't?" they asked in unison.

"Then, who do you like?" asked Jessica.

"I like . . ." Without my meaning them to, my

eyes found Sam standing by the door. He waved at me.

Jessica saw. "You like Sam Wolff? No *way*."

I gave her a tiny smile. "Way," I said.

Jessica considered what I'd said. "But doesn't he just stare at you and not say anything? How can you know you like him?"

I laughed. "He doesn't not say anything."

And then, like a character in a comic strip who suddenly gets an illuminated lightbulb over her head, Jessica shouted, "Oh, I know! It's because you're both into art and stuff." She nodded to emphasize the accuracy of her insight.

"Totally," said Madison, nodding too. She looked over at Sam and narrowed her eyes. Then she looked back at me. "Actually, he's kind of cute," she said.

"Thanks," I said. I let my eyes rest on Sam for a second before turning back to Madison and Jessica. "Well, have fun in the Hamptons."

"I wish you were coming," said Madison. "You have to call us while we're there."

"And you'll come over Sunday night," said Jessica. "So we can debrief."

"Really?" I said, surprised.

"What do you mean, 'really'?" Madison looked confused.

"Yeah," said Jessica. "I mean, we're not going to see you all weekend." She and Madison both hugged me. Before letting go, Jessica gave me one last piece of advice.

"If your stepmother says you can't come Sunday, just tie her up and lock her in the closet."

"I don't think it'll come to that," I said. "I'll see you Sunday."

And as I crossed the ballroom, I felt a tremendous surge of joy. Who knew you could dump your prince and still keep your loyal court?

Outside the wind was whipping a few pale clouds across the sky, which was bright with the nearly full moon. A row of horse-drawn carriages was lined up across the street, waiting to take people on rides through Central Park.

"I can't believe this is happening," Sam said. He took my hand and gestured with it toward the horses. "So, what do you think? Want to ride off into the sunset on a slightly anemic steed?"

I took his other hand in mine and turned him to face me. "Look, you should know. It turns out I don't really have a wicked stepmother," I said. "So I don't believe in fairy tales anymore."

"Really?" He furrowed his forehead. "No magic spells?" I shook my head. "No fairy godmothers?" I shook it again. "What happened? Ding-dong the witch is dead."

I laughed. "She's not dead." I looked across the street, as if the answer to Sam's question was hiding somewhere in the park. When it didn't emerge, I just shrugged. "I don't know," I said. "It's like everything changed but nothing changed, you know what I mean?" Sam shook his head. "Yeah, I don't exactly know either."

Sam put his hands on either side of my face. "Well, anyway, I'm glad," he said. "It must really suck to have a wicked stepmother." He kissed me lightly on the lips. "Then again, I wouldn't have minded being your Prince Charming."

I slipped my arms over his shoulders and touched his soft, curly hair. "Oh, yes you would have," I said.

Sam wrapped his arms around my waist and leaned his forehead against mine. "Well, if you still want to be a princess, that's okay by me."

I considered it for a second. "You know, I think I'll pass," I said.

"Suit yourself," said Sam. And then, just as we were about to kiss, he froze. "Wait, we still get to have the happy ending, right?"

"Oh, definitely," I said, tilting my face up to his. "We *definitely* get to have the happy ending."

I am lucky enough to owe thanks to Ben Gantcher, Neal Gantcher, Elizabeth Rudnick, the Saint Ann's Community, Angie Sheldon, and my extraordinary editor, Helen Perelman.